Temple Israel Library
2324 Emerson Avenue South
Minneapolis, MN. 55405

THE
Atonement
OF
Mindy Wise

Marilyn Kaye

THE
Atonement
O F
Mindy Wise

Gulliver Books
Harcourt Brace Jovanovich, Publishers
San Diego • *New York* • *London*

HBJ

Requests for permission to make copies of any part of
the work should be mailed to: Permissions Department,
Harcourt Brace Jovanovich, Publishers,
Orlando, Florida 32887.

Library of Congress Cataloging-in-Publication Data
Kaye, Marilyn.
The atonement of Mindy Wise/Marilyn Kaye.—1st ed.
p. cm.
"Gulliver books."
Summary: Yom Kippur services let Mindy reflect on the sins
she committed during her thirteenth year, when she was desperately
anxious to get into a popular crowd at her new middle school.
ISBN 0-15-200402-5
[1. Popularity—Fiction. 2. Schools—Fiction. 3. Jews—Fiction.]
I. Title.
PZ7.K2127At   1991
[Fic]—dc20   90-45954

Designed by Camilla Filancia
Printed in the United States of America

First edition   A B C D E

For LAYNE HUDES
and CRAIG KALPAKJIAN,
without guilt

THE
Atonement
OF
Mindy Wise

Chapter 1

I'm hungry. I'm sitting in a synagogue, a house of worship, where I'm supposed to be feeling terribly religious and spiritual, but all I can think about is food and what I'm going to eat when I get out of here. It's not easy being spiritual when visions of pizza are floating through your mind.

Stop it, Mindy, I tell myself. You don't get to eat until sundown, and that's at least eight hours away. You're just torturing yourself. Besides, you're not supposed to be thinking about food. Not today.

Today is Yom Kippur, the holiest day in the Jewish year. Actually, it started last night, because that's how Jewish holidays go, from sundown to sundown. This is the day when Jews are supposed to fast and pray and ask forgiveness for all the sins they committed in the past year.

It's the biggie as far as Jewish holidays go, so the place is packed, lots of families. I'm here alone. Back where we used to live, in New Jersey, my family went to services sometimes, mainly when my grandmother got on my parents' case. But when we moved here, to Fox Haven, Connecticut, a year ago, my parents didn't join a synagogue. They aren't exactly religious. Neither am I for that matter. I dropped out of Hebrew school in second grade because it conflicted with Brownie meetings.

When I told my family last night I wanted to go to services today, my parents didn't object, but they gave each other what I call The Look. It's an expression I've been seeing a lot lately. It involves eye-rolling and twitching lips, like they're trying to hold back smiles. If I had to give it a specific name, I'd call it the "now what's this all about" look. It's very annoying. They were probably thinking this was another one of my phases, like the time I decided to become a vegetarian. That lasted until I had a Big Mac attack. About two days.

At least they didn't start bombarding me with questions. Possibly because I don't think they take anything I say all that seriously. Or maybe it's because my mother's been reading a lot of books and articles lately about getting along with adolescents, and I'll bet they all tell parents not to be too nosy. It's good advice.

My sister, Valerie, who has all the wisdom of a ten-year-old mental midget, thought she understood why I was doing this. Her brilliant conclusion was that I just wanted to get out of chores. I responded with my best withering look, the one I reserve exclusively for her.

I scan the faces of the people around me. They don't look like the kinds of people who have committed a lot of sins. But then, appearances can be deceiving. If they noticed me, they probably wouldn't think I was that awful either. They'd just see a short, dark-haired teenage girl who needs to lose five pounds. Okay, ten. They might not know my name, Mindy Ann Wise, but they'll assume I'm just your basic nice Jewish girl. And they'll think I'm here because this is where nice Jewish girls are supposed to be today.

Well, they'd be partly right. I am a Jewish girl. And I'm fourteen, which definitely makes me a teenager. But they're wrong about the "nice" part, and they're wrong if they think I'm just here because I'm supposed to be here. I'm here so I won't get struck by lightning.

I've gone to Yom Kippur services before. And I know that by the end of this day, it will be decided whether or not I'll be written into the Book of Life for another year. I never paid much attention to that before. I just assumed my name would get in.

This year is different. And if I don't do some major atoning . . . okay, maybe I won't get struck by lightning. But I could drown, or get hit by a car . . . the possibilities are endless. As I consider them, my heart starts thumping.

I'm nervous, I'm hungry, and something else, too. I'm angry. Because it's not really my fault that I'm in this situation. If we'd never moved here, I wouldn't be so worried about atoning for sins. I wouldn't even have committed the sins in the first place. I was never a bad person before.

Fox Haven, Connecticut, turned me into a sinner.

Moving from New Jersey to Connecticut last August didn't seem like a big problem for anyone but me. My parents were happy about the big new house, the nice neighborhood, and all that stuff. They would still be commuting to the same jobs in New York City. Valerie was too immature to care about leaving her friends and her school. I was the one who was suffering.

In all fairness, I had to admit I liked my new room. It had blue walls, a white ceiling, and a closet three times bigger than the one in my old bedroom. Best of all, it was mine, all mine. No more sharing with Valerie.

But there was a major downside to this move. I'd lived in Riverside, New Jersey, all my life. I had friends there, not to mention tons of relatives. I didn't know anyone in Fox Haven. In less than two weeks I would be starting the eighth grade at Fox Haven Middle School where I would be a total stranger, while all the other kids would have been together for two years already.

Two moving men came in with the big mirror that went over my dresser. I watched them attach it. As soon as they left, I stood before it and examined my reflection. How would people see me here?

My new haircut was nice, layered around the face but with enough hanging down the back to gather in a clip. Hair clips were very big back in Riverside, and I had about twenty.

The tan I got at the beach was just about gone, but a little blush would make my skin look better. I made my usual weekly resolution to lose five pounds and thought about what I was going to wear the first day of school.

I envisioned myself entering the homeroom at Fox Haven Middle, wearing my new denim skirt with a red shirt, my hair pulled back with a matching red clip. Then I practiced smiling—not a big, goofy smile, but a small mysterious one, the kind that looks friendly but not pushy, the kind that makes people want to find out who you are.

Examining the smile objectively, I realized it didn't look mysterious at all, just sickly. I tried again, showing a few more teeth this time. Better. Think positive, I ordered my reflection. It's going to be a great year.

Then I watched my smile fade. It was all very

nice fantasizing about the future, two weeks away. Right then, at that very moment, I was bored and lonely. I thought about going through my closet and planning my school outfits for the first month, coordinating them with the hair clips, but that didn't excite me.

I threw myself down onto my bare mattress, stared up at the shiny white ceiling, and allowed a cloud of gloom to descend.

"Mindy, don't lie on the bed with your shoes on."

My mother stood in the doorway. She looked awful. Her hair was all over the place, and there were smudges on her T-shirt. Her mouth was set in a tight line, and she was tapping her foot.

I exhaled a deep, heart-wrenching groan. Then, slowly, I lifted my legs and swung them over to the side.

"And since you don't look very busy," she continued, "how about helping me put kitchen things away."

She was always phrasing sentences like questions but they were really orders. That got on my nerves, and I considered starting an argument but I wasn't in the mood. I dragged myself off the bed. Then something out the window caught my eye.

My window faced the carport of the house next door. I made out the figures of two boys shooting baskets.

I turned back to my mother. "Could I do that later?" I asked. "I was thinking about taking a walk around the neighborhood. Maybe meet some kids . . ."

I waited for my mother to sigh. She sighed a lot, and she had several different kinds of sighs. There was her sad sigh, her mad sigh, and her aggravated sigh, the one I expected to hear that moment. But she surprised me. "That's a good idea. Maybe you'll find someone to go to school with."

That took me aback for a second, until I figured out why she was being so agreeable. I'd made a pretty huge fuss about leaving Riverside, claiming I'd be lonely and friendless and totally miserable in Fox Haven. And for the past forty-eight hours I'd been moping a lot. I knew from experience that the more depressed I acted the nicer they'd all be to me.

I gave my mother a sad-but-hopeful smile. "Maybe." As soon as she turned away, I checked myself again in the mirror. Quickly, I brushed some Rosy Glow across my cheeks and fumbled in my top drawer for a yellow hair clip to go with my T-shirt. I ran down the stairs and out the front door. Then I slowed down to a casual stroll, and made my way around to the side of the house, where I could see the neighbors' carport.

As soon as I had a clear view, I realized my earlier observation was wrong. Only one of the two figures was a boy. But what a boy! He was great looking—

tall with broad shoulders and sandy blond hair . . .
but older, definitely older. At least sixteen, I figured.

The girl tossing the ball to him looked more like
my age. And it was easy to see why I'd made the
mistake from my bedroom window. She was tall and
skinny—no chest whatsoever—and her hair was
shorter than the boy's. She wore shorts and a tank
top that looked pretty sweaty. She had a cute face,
though.

I coughed, and she turned toward me with a big,
easy smile. "Hi! You just move in next door?"

I nodded. "I'm Mindy Wise."

"I'm Peggy Cavanaugh. That's my brother,
Kevin."

Mr. Gorgeous hit me with a smile that knocked
me out. "Hi, Mindy." He tossed the basketball back
to Peggy. "Gotta run. See ya later." I watched him
longingly as he ran into the house.

"Will you be going to the Middle School?" Peggy
asked me.

"Yeah. Eighth grade."

Peggy's smile broadened. "Me too. Hey, you
want a soda?"

"Sure, thanks."

She led me into her house. "Have a seat," she
said, pointing to the kitchen table while she opened
the refrigerator. "We've got Coke, ginger ale, and
orange juice."

"Any diet soda?" I asked.

"No, just regular."

"Okay, I'll have a Coke."

Peggy took two Cokes from the refrigerator. "Are you on a diet?"

"I'm *always* on a diet." I eyed her scrawny legs. "I'll bet you never have to watch what you eat."

"Never," Peggy said cheerfully as she poured the drinks into glasses. "And I eat like a horse. But I'm always running around, playing basketball and doing gymnastics, so I guess I work it off. I'm on the regional gymnastic team. Are you into sports?"

"I *hate* sports." Then, afraid I was sounding awfully rude, I quickly added, "But I really respect athletes. I probably just hate sports because I'm no good at them. I get C's in phys ed."

"Well, you're probably good at a lot of things I'm crummy at," Peggy said, joining me at the table with the sodas. "How are you on book reports and essays?"

"Not bad," I said modestly.

"Great! Let's make a deal. I'll help you in phys ed and you can help me in English."

"It's a deal," I replied.

So Peggy and I started hanging out together. It was strange. She was nothing like any of my friends back home. Sometimes I wondered if I'd be friends with her at all if she didn't live right next door. We had practically nothing in common.

She wasn't a reader, like me. To her, reading was

work, something you did for school, because you *had* to. On a rainy Sunday, she preferred to sit in front of some incredibly boring football game on TV. And she understood what was going on. She tried to explain it to me once, but I told her very honestly that I wasn't the least bit interested in football. She wasn't offended.

In fact, it seemed impossible to offend her. When I tactfully suggested that she might consider letting her hair grow (it really looked awful), she just shrugged and said it was easier for gymnastics to keep it short. When I realized she hadn't started shaving her legs yet, I was totally floored and probably showed it. But she didn't care. She just said she'd get around to it one of these days, and it was no big deal.

We were definitely opposites. I was dying to see the Fox Haven Mall, but Peggy was never up for that. "What's the point?" she said. "It's just a bunch of stores." When I asked her what the kids at Fox Haven wore, she said she'd never really noticed—all she ever wore to school was jeans. The kind with no label. And when I tried on two different eyeshadows for her and asked her which looked better, she said she couldn't tell the difference.

No, Peggy wasn't someone I'd ever have chosen to be friends with. But she was nice and easygoing. Besides, I didn't have any choice. If it wasn't for Peggy, I would have gone crazy from boredom.

And even if she wasn't very cool, she could be fun. I got her to start watching "All My Children," my favorite soap opera, and she got into it. We'd have these intense conversations about the characters, analyzing their behavior and guessing what they were going to do next. And Peggy liked music videos, so we watched a lot of those. That was one thing we had in common. We both knew all the words to the songs, so we sang along with the TV.

Mostly we just hung out, at her place or mine. Mine was better because we had cable, and my parents both worked so we could watch TV all day and no one hassled us. Ms. Hitch, the woman who came in to clean and make sure Valerie didn't burn the house down, left us alone as long as we didn't make a mess.

But her place had its advantages, too. Her mother was a fantastic cook, and there were always goodies in the kitchen—brownies, fancy cookies, cakes. Then there was always the possibility of a glimpse of Kevin. Not that he ever paid much attention to me. He'd breeze in and out with a "hiya, girls" and flash that incredible smile, but that was about it. I was amazed when he actually offered to take us out one evening.

It was just after dinner, and I'd gone over to Peggy's to play a new video game with her. Her parents were out for the evening, and we were in the family room in front of the TV when Kevin stuck his head in.

"I'm going out for ice cream. You kids want to come?"

I winced at his calling us kids, but the invitation

was worth the insult. I almost kicked Peggy when she pointed out to him that there was ice cream in the freezer.

"Yeah, I know," he said, "but there's no hot fudge. And I've got a major craving for a hot fudge sundae."

"Mmmm," I moaned, "I *love* hot fudge sundaes. C'mon, Peggy, let's go."

"But I'm winning," Peggy complained. Even so, she agreed. We all piled into the front seat of their mother's car and drove to the Soda Shoppe.

I'd never been there before, but I'd passed it and looked through the windows. It was designed to look like an old-fashioned place, with white tables and chairs and waitresses wearing cutesy striped outfits with ruffles. It was always crowded.

I should have known Kevin had an ulterior motive in going there. The minute we walked in, he smiled at one particular waitress.

"Kevin!" she said. "What are you doing here?"

He cocked his head to one side, indicating us. "The kids were begging for ice cream."

Peggy and I exchanged meaningful looks.

"Well, I'm just about to go on break," the waitress said. They went off to sit together at a cozy table in the corner, while Peggy and I found a spot on the opposite side of the room.

"Is that his girlfriend?" I asked Peggy.

"One of zillions, probably," Peggy replied. "Yuck, they're getting mushy."

I sneaked a peek. Sure enough, they were holding hands, and their heads were pressed almost close enough to kiss. Unlike Peggy, however, I wasn't thinking "yuck."

Another ruffled waitress came to take our order. Despite my earnest resolve to lose five pounds before school started, I ordered a hot fudge sundae. I figured if I skipped two meals a day for the next week I could make up for it. Then, while Peggy ordered, I looked around the room.

I saw three girls sitting around a table. Their heads were huddled together, and I couldn't hear them, but at one point two of them shrieked, "Oh Dani, you *didn't!*" Then one of them looked around as if to make sure no one had heard them.

When she saw us, she sort of smiled and nodded at Peggy. Peggy smiled back, and then turned her attention to the banana split that had appeared before her.

"Who are those girls?" I asked, as I spooned hot fudge over my ice cream.

"They're from school," she said. "Lisa Molinari, Dani Dixon, and Marsha Something."

"You mean, they're going into the eighth grade?"

Peggy nodded. Covertly, I turned and looked them over. I'd thought they were older. Maybe it was their clothes. One of them was all in black—black jeans, black tank top, dangling black earrings. Even her hair was black, long and straight. Another wore an oversize T-shirt, knotted at the hip, over a short short skirt. She had short brown hair, curly. The third wore adorable flowered overalls. They all could have been models in *Seventeen*.

"Are they friends of yours?" Even as I asked the question, I knew the answer from the offhand way the girl had greeted Peggy.

"Not really. I mean, I wouldn't call them enemies. But we don't hang out together."

It occurred to me that Peggy didn't hang out with anyone, besides me. "Who *are* your friends?"

Peggy considered this. "Well, there's Quentin. He was in science with me last year, and we got to be pretty good buddies. He's on vacation with his parents. And there's Karen, but she's off at summer camp."

Only two friends? My expression must have told Peggy I found that peculiar, because she immediately offered an explanation.

"Most of my friends are on the gymnastics team. The center is in Crawford, about twenty miles from here, so they go to Crawford Middle."

That set her off on a description of her latest adventures on the vault and the balance beam and the parallel bars. While she talked, I took another sidelong glance at the three girls. So that's what eighth graders at Fox Haven Middle School looked like. I wanted to sink under the table. Here I was, in faded shorts and a shirt I'd had since I was eleven. Peggy looked just as bad in her baggy cutoffs.

We both looked like nerds. But Peggy, being Peggy, probably didn't care.

I did.

That's where it all began—sitting with Peggy in the Soda Shoppe, and looking at those three girls. And because of what that led to, I'm sitting here now in the synagogue, worried about whether or not I'll get into the Book of Life.

The congregation's rising. I look at my prayer book and see a whole list of sins. It's time to start confessing and asking for forgiveness. But for me to do that, I have to pick out the sins I committed. Which means I have to think about them. This is the part I've been dreading. It's at times like this I wish I didn't have such a good memory.

Chapter 2

For the sin which we have committed before Thee by wronging our neighbor . . .

On the morning of the first day of school, I stood before the mirror and gave myself a cold, hard, critical once-over. After trying on five different outfits, I'd settled on my original choice—the denim skirt with the red shirt. Slowly, I pivoted, keeping my head over my shoulder to catch my reflection from every possible angle. The profile was the worst. I sucked in my stomach and saw a minor improvement.

There was a light knock on the door. "Mindy?"

I exhaled. "Come on in, Mom."

She stood in the doorway. "Don't you want any breakfast?"

"I'm not hungry."

As her eyes took in the clothes scattered all over the floor, a sigh escaped her lips. But at least she didn't start nagging. Every now and then, she could be sensitive to my mood.

"All ready for your first day? You look very nice."

Now I was worried. The last time my mother and I agreed on the way I looked, I was about six years old. "I don't even know if they're wearing denim skirts here."

"What does that matter as long as you like what you're wearing? Mindy, don't worry so much about what everybody else does. Just be yourself, and you'll be fine."

I rolled my eyes, but I kept my mouth shut. My mother obviously had no idea what went on in middle schools. But this was no time to begin instructing her.

"How come you didn't leave with Dad?" They usually drove together to the station for the train to New York.

"I'm taking Valerie to her school. Are you sure you don't want me to come with you, too?"

I couldn't imagine anything more humiliating than walking into school on the first day with your mother. "No thanks. Peggy's coming over to walk with me."

"That's nice." She came closer and brushed a curl off my forehead. I promptly pulled it back. She sighed. It was a ritual we went through. "You're lucky to have already made a good friend like Peggy, even before school's started."

"Mmm." Peggy might not be the most exciting companion in the world, but at least I wouldn't be facing the unknown alone. The thought of having my down-to-earth, practical neighbor by my side was comforting.

Valerie burst into my room. "Mom, come on!"

"I'm coming. Doesn't Mindy look nice, Val?"

Valerie made a gagging noise. Since that was her usual reaction to my appearance, it didn't bother me.

My mother seemed reluctant to leave. "You're sure Peggy's coming?"

I nodded. That was one thing I didn't have to worry about. Peggy was very reliable. Sure enough, at that very moment the doorbell rang.

"I'll let her in on our way out," my mother said. She made one last attempt to adjust my hair.

"Mom!"

"Okay, okay! Have a good day."

When Peggy walked in, I didn't even bother with the usual greetings. "How do I look?"

"Fine," Peggy said. That didn't exactly bolster my ego. She always said that. "We better get going. Don't you have to be there early to pick up your schedule?"

"Yeah, let me just pick out some shoes." As I rummaged in my closet, I took a quick look at what Peggy was wearing. Not that I expected it to provide me with any guidelines. Peggy just wasn't into clothes. I could have predicted she'd be wearing plain jeans and a short-sleeved polo shirt. "Should I wear flats or sandals?"

"I don't know," Peggy said. "Whatever you like."

"Well, what do the kids at Fox Haven wear? Flats or sandals?"

"I guess I never really noticed," Peggy replied. She grinned. "I don't go around looking at people's feet."

Flats were a safer bet. I slipped them on, grabbed my purse and my three-ring notebook, and we took off. As we walked to school, I told her about the nightmare I had last night. "I couldn't find my classroom. I was running all through this building looking for it, for days and days. And when I finally found it, they were taking the final exam. And I flunked."

With some kids, I would have been embarrassed to tell a dream like that. But I knew Peggy wouldn't laugh at me. "Don't worry, I'll make sure you don't get lost."

When we entered the school, it was still early. Only a few kids were roaming the halls, along with some teachers pushing trolleys loaded with textbooks.

The place was a maze, with corridors branching off in every possible direction. Peggy led me through hallways, pointing out the cafeteria, the library, the rest rooms. "Here's the office," she announced.

I followed her into the large room. There seemed to be a dozen people in there, shuffling papers and slamming file drawers. One woman was stapling papers together behind a desk. I watched in wonder as she kept up a perfect rhythm, her head bobbing in time with the stapler.

My stomach was churning. I had no idea which of these people to approach. I was eternally grateful when Peggy took charge.

"Mrs. Andrews?"

The woman looked up, holding the stapler in midair. I had a fleeting image of her shooting a staple right between my eyes.

"This is Mindy Wise," Peggy said. "She's new. Do you have her schedule?"

The woman glared at me, as if she was trying to decide whether I was really and truly Mindy Wise. I stepped back. But Peggy faced her directly. "She got a letter saying she was supposed to pick up her schedule here. Show her the letter, Mindy." She spoke as if I was a little kid, but I didn't mind one bit.

I pulled it out of my purse, handed it to the dragon lady behind the desk, and tried to look friendly. The woman glanced at the letter and thrust it back at me. Then she jerked open a file drawer, flipped through it, and pulled out a sheet of paper. Wordlessly, she gave it to me. Then she resumed her stapling.

"Okay, let's see." Peggy peered over my shoulder. "You've got homeroom Eight B, in room three twenty-eight."

"Where's three twenty-eight?"

"I'll show you." Then she pulled out her own schedule to compare them.

I looked at them both in dismay. "We don't have any of the same classes!"

"Yeah, I know. But we've got the same lunch period, so we can have lunch together."

That was a relief. One of my biggest fears was the idea of eating alone in the cafeteria. Then I clutched my throat. "But how am I going to find the cafeteria?"

"You'll see a whole bunch of people going in the same direction. Just follow them. Relax! There are three hundred kids at this school. You can always ask directions."

At that moment, I absolutely loved Peggy. I could tell she thought my fears were silly, but she didn't make fun of them. We left the office and went back into the hallway. By now there were more kids milling around. I spotted a couple of denim skirts almost exactly like mine and started to calm down.

I followed Peggy up a flight of stairs, and down another hall. "Here you are," she announced. "Room three twenty-eight. And I'll meet you at lunch."

"How will I find you?" I pictured hundreds of kids racing around with trays, and me just standing there, frantically searching for the one face I knew.

Another person might have told me just to keep my eyes open and look. But Peggy checked my schedule. "You've got phys ed right before lunch. Why don't I meet you right outside the exit from the girls' locker room?"

"Great. I'll see you later."

Peggy gave me a reassuring smile and took off. I took a deep breath and walked into my homeroom.

It was still early, so there weren't many kids inside. My eyes rested on a girl sitting toward the back, flipping through a magazine.

She was cute, with short, blondish brown hair in a Princess Diana style, and she was wearing cropped pants. She didn't look nervous, like a new person, but she didn't look snobby either. So I made my way down an aisle and slid into the seat next to hers.

She glanced at me and offered something that resembled a smile. That gave me the courage to speak. "Hi. Is this Eight B?"

"Yeah." Her eyes returned to the magazine. She was studying a page of fashions. I leaned over and took a look.

"I like that outfit," I said.

She shrugged. "It's okay. I'm not crazy about the top."

"No, I don't like the top either," I said quickly. "Um, I'm Mindy Wise."

Now she actually turned to me. "I'm Kelly Barker. Are you new?"

"Yeah. We just moved here from New Jersey."

"Oh."

Then there was silence. I had a zillion questions I wanted to ask her, only I couldn't think of even one that wouldn't sound stupid. But I was spared the need to continue the conversation. As the room started to fill, two girls came in and sat just in back of us. Kelly immediately turned around and greeted them with joy.

I recognized one of them from the Soda Shoppe, but I couldn't remember her name. And Kelly didn't bother to introduce me. I pretended I wasn't listening to them, but of course I was.

"How was Dani's party?" Kelly asked them.

"Just so-so, but don't tell her I said that," the one from the Soda Shoppe said. "Hardly anyone was there. I guess most of the kids were still away."

"How come you weren't at the mall Saturday?" Kelly asked the other one.

The girl pushed her thin blond bangs out of her eyes and sighed. "I had to go with my parents to visit my grandmother in New Haven. We always go there, the first Saturday of every month."

Here was an opening for me, and I couldn't resist. "I used to have to do that, too. When we lived in New Jersey. We went almost every Sunday to see my grandparents."

The two girls looked at me blankly. But Kelly came through. "This is Mindy. She's new." She indicated the one from the Soda Shoppe. "This is Lisa. And that's Gayle."

"Hi," the two girls chorused. They looked almost friendly. I was hoping to get more conversation going, but the teacher walked in.

The next half hour was taken up with all the usual

first-day-of-school homeroom stuff—roll call, tons of forms to fill out, the standard welcome speech from the principal over the intercom. Behind me, I could hear Lisa and Gayle whispering, and occasionally, when the teacher wasn't looking, Kelly turned and added something. I didn't say anything, though. The worst thing a new girl can be is pushy.

When the bell rang, the two girls behind me flew out of the room. I looked at my schedule. Spanish, in the language lab. My stomach lurched. Where was the language lab? Luckily, Kelly had stayed to retie the laces on her tennis shoes, and she noticed my distress. "What's your next class?"

"Spanish. Language lab."

"Me too." She got up, and paused. I accepted this as an invitation to walk with her. We didn't say much along the way. I complimented her on the color of her high-tops (turquoise) and made a mental note to wear my pink ones tomorrow. Kelly kept stopping to greet people, and sometimes she'd introduce me.

When we reached the language lab, Kelly paused in the doorway and surveyed the occupants. She seemed to be trying to decide who she wanted to sit near. Apparently, she didn't see anyone interesting, because she took a seat at the end of a row. I took the empty seat next to her.

There was no teacher there yet. I watched Kelly hopefully. Finally, she spoke. "It must be hard being new."

I nodded. "It is. I mean, back in Riverside I knew everyone. (Lie.) I don't know anyone here. Except Peggy Cavanaugh. She lives next door."

"I don't know her," Kelly said.

The bell rang, but still no teacher appeared. Just then, the awful woman from the office ran in, looking more harried than before. She addressed the class. "There's been a problem with scheduling," she announced, glaring at us as if it was our fault. "A teacher will be coming soon. So just stay quiet and study on your own." She ran out of the room.

What were we supposed to study when school hadn't even started yet? I turned back to Kelly. "Those girls in our homeroom seem nice. Are they friends of yours?"

"Sort of," Kelly said. She looked around, as if to make sure no one was listening. No one was, but she lowered her voice anyway. "See, there's this group of girls, Lisa and Gayle and Dani Dixon and some others. They've got this club, called The Club."

"What kind of club?" I asked.

Kelly shrugged. "It's just a club. They started it last year. They have parties, and they hang out at the mall on Saturday. I hang out with them sometimes, and other kids do, too, but we're not actual members. Some of the things they do are just for members."

"Do they ever let new members in?"

"Yeah, last spring they had this rush party, just like at a college. And they picked new girls. Janet

Peterson and Marsha Greene got in. They'll have another rush party this spring."

"Do you think you're going to get in this spring?"

Kelly bit her lip. "I hope so. But lots of other girls want to get in, too."

The teacher walked in just then, so we had to stop talking. It was funny that Peggy had never mentioned The Club to me. If it was that important, she must know about it. And I could tell from Kelly's respectful tone that it *was* important.

Spanish class was okay. It mostly consisted of turning to your neighbor and asking, *"Como esta usted?"* and your neighbor replying, *"Muy bien, gracias, y usted?"* Afterwards, Kelly pointed me toward my algebra class. I didn't see anyone interesting in there, which was good because I had to concentrate. I could tell algebra was going to be brutal.

After that came phys ed, my most dreaded class. We didn't have to change because it was the first day. We were given our gym clothes (horrible blue one-piece things), assigned lockers, and gathered on the gym bleachers to listen to a lecture on teamwork and sportsmanship.

I spotted Gayle, one of the girls from my homeroom, and waved to her. I was very pleased when she waved back. And I was even happier when I found that she had the locker right next to mine.

I was hoping we'd talk when we were putting

our gym suits in the lockers, but she was deep in conversation with a tall girl who had frizzy red hair. "Can you go to the skating rink after school?" she asked her.

"Yeah, probably," the redhead replied. "I'm supposed to be grounded, but I think I can get out of it."

Gayle laughed. "Oh, Flip, what did you do this time?"

Flip grinned. "I put my red slippers in the wash with the baby clothes. Now my poor little baby brother's all in pink."

I would have laughed along with them, but then they'd know I was eavesdropping and might think I was nosy. I watched them go off together, and I figured this Flip person must be a Club member, too.

Peggy was waiting for me outside the locker room, just as she promised. "How's it going?" she asked as we walked to the cafeteria.

"Okay," I said. "I heard all about The Club."

"Which club?"

"Just something called The Club. There's a girl named Gayle in it, and Dani, and Lisa. And someone called Flip."

"Oh, that's Philippa Duval," Peggy said. "Yeah, I guess you'd call that the in crowd." There wasn't the slightest note of envy in her voice. It was as if she didn't find The Club of any interest whatsoever.

The cafeteria wasn't much different from the one

in my old school—noisy and crowded. I stuck close to Peggy. Somehow, I found myself with a tray in my hand being led to a table.

"Mindy, this is Quentin Poole and Karen Ziegler. This is my new neighbor, Mindy Wise."

An owlish-looking boy with big ears stared at me and nodded. Karen smiled, exposing a mouthful of silver. That was the only thing about her that wasn't mousy. Everything else—from her dull stringy hair to her plain white shirt—was pretty bland. Basically, she looked like she was about ten years old.

She was nice enough, I guess. She asked me how I liked Fox Haven and my classes. Quentin didn't say much.

Karen started talking about summer camp. She had gone to one of these computer camps, and I didn't understand what she was talking about. I let my eyes wander around the room. Way over on the other side, I saw some of those girls from The Club. They took over one whole long table. I couldn't hear them, but I could see they were laughing. Other kids stopped by their table to talk. Some of them were boys—cute ones. Other kids just waved as they passed.

No one stopped by our table. No one waved to us either. I'd already figured out that Peggy wasn't the social type. Obviously, neither were Karen and Quentin. I acted like I was listening to Karen's recital of camp events, but I kept sneaking peeks at that other table.

For the rest of the day, in each of my classes, I kept my eyes open for those girls and listened for their names in roll call. One of them—Dani Dixon—appeared in my social studies class. She was really cute, petite, with curly brown hair and the greenest eyes I'd ever seen. She showed up in English, too, sitting with a girl named Marsha. In my last class, science, I saw Flip, the red-haired girl from phys ed. I took a seat next to her.

The science teacher was talking about what we'd be doing that term. "Be thinking about pairing up for lab partners," he said. "Next month, we'll be dissecting frogs." I felt my stomach turn over.

"Gross," I muttered. At the same time, Flip said, "Gross." We looked at each other and grinned. When the bell rang, she turned to me. "Want to be lab partners?" she asked. "I don't want to get stuck with someone who *likes* cutting up frogs."

I agreed happily.

Walking home with Peggy that afternoon, I said, "Those Club girls seem pretty cool."

Peggy didn't share my opinion. "I always thought they were kind of snobby."

"I'm sure they're nice when you get to know them," I said.

Peggy made a face. "I don't like Dani Dixon. We had a girl in class last year who stuttered when she talked. Dani made fun of her."

"That's not nice," I admitted. "But just because

one of the girls is mean doesn't mean the whole crowd's bad."

"Maybe," Peggy said. "I guess I just don't know them. They just don't seem like the kind of people I'd want to hang out with. They act like they think they're really cool."

Because they probably are, I replied silently. I found it very hard to believe anyone would prefer the company of Karen and Quentin.

As if she was reading my mind, Peggy asked, "How do you like Quentin and Karen?"

"They seem very nice," I said politely.

"Yeah, they're okay," Peggy agreed. "I've known them since kindergarten. We're not really super-close friends, but it's nice having people to eat lunch with."

"But you could eat with other people, too, couldn't you? If you wanted to?"

Peggy shrugged. "Most of the kids at school are in cliques. They've been sitting with the same people since last year. Besides, what's the point? It's just a thirty-minute lunch period. What difference does it make who you sit with?"

I gazed at her in amazement. How could she be so unconscious?

Peggy misinterpreted my expression. "Don't get me wrong, I'm glad you're sitting with us now. I know Quentin can be awfully quiet, and sometimes Karen goes on and on about things no one else is interested in. It'll be more fun having you there."

I smiled, but her words had struck an ominous chord. Were lunch groups that firmly established? Was I destined to have lunch with Karen and Quentin for my entire time at Fox Haven Middle School?

As the days went by, Fox Haven Middle School started becoming more familiar territory. It got so I could get to my classes without thinking "make a left here" and looking for the door numbers.

I was lonely, though. I wasn't seeing Peggy as much as I had before school started. We walked to school together in the mornings, but she had gymnastics almost every day after school, and her mother picked her up. I still sat with her and Quentin and Karen at lunch, but they were always talking about stuff I didn't find very interesting, like Peggy's practices or Quentin's chess matches. Karen talked about her pen pals. I didn't know anyone over the age of ten had pen pals. I spent most of the half hour every day looking at that other table across the room.

I was starting to get to know some of those girls. In homeroom, I heard Lisa, Gayle, and Kelly talking about a movie I'd seen, so I joined the conversation. They didn't seem to mind.

In phys ed, I was on the same volleyball team with Flip and Gayle. Flip was good at volleyball, so I asked her if she'd help me practice serving. She was pretty nice about it. In another week or so, we'd start being lab partners in science, and I hoped that would be an opportunity to get to know her better.

Marsha, in English, was sick one day, and I loaned her my notes to copy. She told me if I was ever absent I could borrow hers.

I couldn't say I was actually becoming friends with any of them. No one had asked for my telephone number, or anything like that.

Peggy was right about one of them. Dani Dixon. She wasn't friendly at all. She was in two of my classes, but in three weeks she'd never said a word to me. When I tried to talk to her one day, she gave me a cold look. Her eyes were ice blue.

Wait a minute. "Excuse me," I said to her. "Maybe I'm crazy, but I could have sworn you have green eyes. And today they're blue."

She looked at me scornfully. "Haven't you ever heard of tinted contacts?"

"Oh! Wow! That's neat." Maybe I was too enthusiastic. She turned away and didn't say another word to me.

About three weeks after school started, Peggy made an announcement at lunch. "I've got my first major gymnastics meet on Saturday. If you guys want to come, my parents will drive you to Crawford." The way she spoke, I could tell this must be a big deal.

"Oh, I can't," Karen said. "I'm really sorry, but I've got an orthodontist appointment. And there's no way I can get out of it."

"I've got a chess game every Saturday," Quentin mumbled.

Peggy accepted their excuses without comment, but I could tell she was disappointed.

"I guess I can come," I said.

Peggy's eyes brightened. "Great!"

I couldn't say I was wild about the prospect of spending a Saturday at a gymnastics meet. But it wasn't like I had anything else to do. And I knew if the roles were reversed, Peggy would do something like that for me.

Then something happened. I was walking out of my science class with Flip, when Gayle came up to us. Or to Flip, actually. "Listen, in case I forget, I need a ride to the mall Saturday. Can your mother pick me up?"

"Sure," Flip said.

"Do you have a nice mall here?" I asked them.

"It's fabulous," Gayle stated. "I can't believe you haven't been there yet. We go every Saturday."

I bent down to pull on my shoes. "I was thinking of going there Saturday."

"We always meet at the record store around noon," Flip said.

Was that an invitation? It had to be! Why else would she have told me the time and place?

Back at my old school in Riverside, there were girls like Flip and Gayle and the rest of The Club. I barely knew them. My girlfriend Cathy and I always wondered how they got to be the kind of girls they were. I mean, we could copy their hairstyles, or their clothes, or whatever, but we'd never be one of them. Cathy once said that maybe when they were born a fairy godmother touched them with a magic wand and said, "Poof! You will be popular." At least, there didn't seem to be any logical explanation.

At dinner that evening, I asked if someone could take me to the mall on Saturday.

"I could drop you on my way to the supermarket," my mother said. "Can Peggy's mother pick you up there to bring you home?"

"I'm not going with Peggy," I said. "I'm meeting some other kids from school." Before she could respond, I asked, "Mom, how are things at work? Do you still have that awful secretary?"

I didn't even listen as she launched into her reply. Peggy. The gymnastics meet. I'd forgotten all about it.

Back in Riverside, if I'd been invited to do something with the popular girls, and I had to break plans with Cathy, she would have understood. But Peggy wouldn't. I was going to have to lie.

I did it just as we arrived at school the next day. "I'm really sorry, but I have to do stuff for my mother on Saturday."

It was a pretty lame excuse. And I could hear real disappointment in Peggy's voice when she said, "Oh, that's too bad."

"Yeah, really. But I'll come to the next one. See ya at lunch."

34

When lunchtime came around, I went to the cafeteria, got my tray, and started toward my usual table. Peggy wasn't there yet, just Karen and Quentin. I dreaded the thought of sitting alone with them, listening to their boring conversation about chess and pen pals.

As I passed the table where The Club girls were sitting, I paused. There was an empty seat right next to Flip. Flip glanced up, grinned, and said, "Hi." It just felt natural for me to take the seat. I did get one "what do you think you're doing" look from Dani, but no one else seemed to mind.

Then I saw Peggy.

She had just come out of the cafeteria line. Our eyes met. She smiled and waved. I smiled back. She stood there for a moment, as if waiting for me to jump up and join her. I looked down and started counting the peas in my chicken pie. When I looked up again, Peggy was gone.

I realized Dani had been watching. "Is she a friend of yours?"

I jumped. "Who?"

"Peggy Cavanaugh." It was amazing how she managed to reveal her opinion of Peggy just by saying her name.

Yes, she's my friend, I was thinking. But that wasn't what I said. "She—she lives next door. That's how I know her."

"Oh." Dani went back to the story she'd been

telling. I stuck a fork into my french fries and felt shallow and small.

Very slowly, I turned and looked at Peggy, now sitting at her table. She was looking at me. Sometimes it's not so great having twenty-twenty vision. I could see everything she was feeling all over her face.

Well, there was no law that stated you had to sit at the same table all the time, despite what Peggy had said. Sometimes I'd sit here. Sometimes I'd sit with Peggy.

That sounded like the right thing to do. But I always knew when I was telling myself a lie. This one was a whopper.

Chapter 3

For the sin which we have committed before Thee by spurning parents . . .

I hated my clothes. Okay, I didn't hate *all* of them. I liked the long print skirt and oversize sweater my grandmother bought me last year. My mother didn't like that outfit, and every time I wore it, I got her sigh of despair, along with the closed eyes and the shaking head that seemed to say, "Oh, Mindy, I can't bear to look at you."

My wardrobe had been okay back in Riverside, but here in Fox Haven it was the pits. After two months at school, I realized how wrong my clothes were.

Back in Riverside, we all bought our clothes at two particular shops, which meant we all looked pretty much the same. In Fox Haven, kids didn't do that. The Club girls didn't even dress alike. Flip, for example, was a little punky. Gayle did a sixties sort of thing, tie-dyed shirts and battered jeans. Marsha and Janet were preppy. Lisa wore black all the time—

it was her trademark. And Dani was elegant, totally coordinated and pulled together.

They had unique styles. Me—I had no style whatsoever. And I had no hope of cultivating one because I had practically no say when it came to buying clothes. My mother always shopped with me, and she wouldn't let me pick out my own things.

Of course, if I made an enormous stink, I didn't have to accept what she selected. But since I didn't like anything she liked, our shopping trips were constant battles, and half the time I'd end up with nothing at all.

Late one Sunday afternoon, I stood in front of my open closet and surveyed the contents with despair.

"Mindy? Could you come down here?" my mother called.

With one last hostile glance at my dreary clothes, I left my room and went down to the living room. Mom and Dad had just returned from the mall, and they were dropping bags on the floor. My father fell into an armchair and picked up the newspaper.

Valerie came tearing up from the basement rec room. "Did you get me anything?"

She was handed a bag and peered inside. "Underpants. Big deal."

"Mindy, look what I found for you." My mother reached into a bag and pulled out a dress.

I didn't even try to hide my dismay. Blue and red

vertical stripes with a white collar. It looked like something a little kid would wear to Sunday school.

"Mom!"

"What?"

"It's not me!"

My mother gave her sigh of exasperation. "What
do you mean, it's not you. What's you?"

I didn't have the slightest idea. But this thing
definitely wasn't.

My mother turned to my father. "George, isn't
this a lovely dress?"

As if my father had any sense of fashion. But he
raised his head, peered at it, and pronounced it
"gorgeous."

"Gorgeous for a ten-year-old, maybe," I said.
"Nobody my age wears dresses like this."

"Somebody must," my father replied. "Or they
wouldn't make them, would they?"

He was always so calm and reasonable. It drove
me crazy.

"Aren't you even going to say thank you?" he
asked mildly. "Your mother spent a lot of time choosing that dress."

"Thank you. Now can you return it?"

"I can't return it," my mother said briskly. "It
was on sale. Now go try it on."

Grimly, I took the dress and went upstairs.
Maybe when she saw it on me, she'd realize how
infantile this dress was. I pulled off my jeans and shirt

and pulled the dress over my head. Then I took a long, hard look at myself. Boring.

I went back downstairs and presented myself. My father nodded with approval. "Very nice."

"And those stripes are slimming," my mother added. "Doesn't Mindy look nice, Val?"

My little sister was on her way back down to the rec room, but she paused to give me a brief examination. "She looks gross." For once, I agreed with her.

"Mom, I hate it!" I wailed.

My father looked up from his paper with a mild expression of annoyance. "Don't talk to your mother like that."

My mother looked less perturbed. She was more accustomed to hearing me throw fits. She picked up the other bags and started up the stairs. "Mindy, you'd say that even if you loved it. You're just being negative."

"You don't understand!" I yelled, following her into her bedroom. "*I* know what I like! Why won't you let me buy my own clothes, by myself?"

"Because I know what you'd end up buying," she said, tossing the bags on the bed.

"Mom, I'm thirteen years old!" By now, I was shrieking. And I could see those tight lines forming on my mother's forehead. Time to switch tactics.

I bowed my head and stared at the floor. If I could keep my eyes open without blinking for sixty seconds, a few tears would form. "Mom . . . I'm not a child anymore." For good measure, I threw in a sniffle.

Unfortunately, my mother was immune to my talents. "Mindy, remember when we went shopping last month, and you wanted to get that shirt? The shoulder seams were hanging down by your elbows! And that jersey dress you wanted. It was so tight you couldn't breathe!"

"But I was going to lose five pounds, and then it would have fit perfectly!" I protested. "Mom, all the girls I know buy their own clothes! *Please*, can't I go shopping on my own?"

My mother cocked her head to one side and gazed at me. For one brief shining moment, I actually thought she might be considering it.

"Mindy, you need a haircut."

I clutched my head protectively and backed away. "I'm letting it grow out."

"Honey, you're too short for long hair. You look so much better with a cute little layered cut."

A cute little layered cut. It was all too much to bear. "You don't care if I'm miserable, do you?" I yelled. "You treat me like a baby! You think I'm too stupid to do anything for myself!" I fled her room and ran across the hall to my own. Flinging myself onto the bed, I buried my face in the pillow.

A few seconds later, I heard her approach my doorway. I didn't lift my head until I heard her sigh. I knew that sigh. It was the "what am I going to do with you" sigh, which frequently comes right before the "I give up" sigh.

"Mindy, look at me." Slowly, I sat up and looked at her.

"I'm going to give you a chance. You can go shopping. I'll give you the money, and you can pick out some clothes. But there are two conditions."

I waited.

"Number one. You can't go alone." She held up a hand to ward off any protest. "Mindy, you're my daughter and I know how your mind works. You'll look in a mirror and get so carried away with a pretty color you won't even notice that there's a hole in the sweater."

I couldn't deny that. She was right. I'm not very detail-oriented. "What if I go with some friends?"

"Peggy?"

"No. Some other friends. What's the second condition?"

"The second condition is that I have to approve of everything you buy. And if I don't like it, you'll have to return it."

My heart sank. That wasn't a condition. It was a catch. She'd never like anything I liked. "But, Mom," I whined.

"Take it or leave it." There were no sighs this time, which meant further discussion was out of the question.

Well, at least I'd get the shopping trip.

"Okay," I said. "It's a deal. Can I go tomorrow? It's a teachers' work day so there's no school."

She agreed. As soon as she left, I sat down on my bed and considered who I should call. I couldn't believe my mother suggested Peggy. Hadn't she ever noticed how Peggy dressed?

Of course, to be fair, maybe she'd forgotten. Peggy didn't come around much anymore. It had been almost three weeks since I stopped sitting with her at lunch. We still walked to school together, though. And she came over and kept me company one night when my parents were out and Valerie was at a sleepover.

She never said anything about my desertion. Mostly, we talked about classes, school projects, and what we saw on television the night before. There were certain topics that we avoided—like my new friends.

Maybe I shouldn't really call them friends yet. This would be the first time I'd called any of them. Even though I'd been eating lunch with them for a month and meeting them most Saturdays at the mall, they hadn't become great buddies. I was still on the fringe. This shopping trip could be more than just a chance to buy clothes. It might be a way of getting closer.

Flip had announced at lunch Friday that she was grounded again, this time for making long-distance phone calls to a boy she met on vacation over the summer. So I decided on Janet, who was pretty friendly and dressed great. I looked up Janet's number in the school directory, went down to the kitchen, and dialed.

"Hi, Janet? This is Mindy."

"Oh. Hi."

I could tell that she was surprised to be hearing from me.

"Listen, I want to go shopping tomorrow for some new clothes. Could you go with me? I really need some help picking out stuff."

"Okay."

"And maybe Lisa could come, too."

"Yeah, I'll call her."

I didn't tell her this was the first time I'd been allowed to pick out my own clothes. And I didn't tell her that everything we bought would probably be returned. I wasn't sure how I'd explain when they eventually asked why I wasn't wearing any of the clothes we bought.

But maybe they'd understand. They probably didn't get along with their mothers either.

I got to the mall first. I waited for the others in front of the record store, which had become the regular meeting place. It seemed like ages to me, but it was only a few minutes before I saw Janet and Lisa coming up the escalator.

From a distance, I admired them. They looked so different, but they both looked so right. Lisa, as usual, was in black—black jeans, black T-shirt, black high-tops. With her long straight black hair, she looked very hip. Janet's jeans were blue like mine, only lighter and not as baggy, and she wore a crisp blue plaid shirt.

I waved to them, and they joined me. "Look," I said, and opened my purse, exposing the contents of my wallet. They were suitably impressed. "What are you going to get?" Lisa asked.

"I haven't the slightest idea," I replied. "That's why I need your help. I want a whole new look."

Janet's eyes swept my body, and she nodded approvingly. "That's a good idea."

I didn't think I looked *that* bad. But I forced a smile. "I want something different, something that's really me. I figured you guys could give me ideas. I mean, you both have such distinctive styles."

They both looked a little embarrassed. I had thought flattery would be appropriate, but I worried that I'd gone too far. Did they think I was going to copy them?

"I'm not going to wear black," I assured Lisa. "My mother doesn't think it's right at my age." Uh-oh. Had I insulted her?

But Lisa wasn't offended. "Yeah, my mother hates the way I dress. But I don't care. She's got no style at all."

"Neither does mine," I said. "Anyway, I probably wouldn't look good in black."

Janet was scrutinizing me thoughtfully. "No, not black. Navy, maybe, or a really dark green."

"You think so?" I asked doubtfully. Red and purple were more what I had in mind. I'd always had a fantasy of looking like a gypsy.

"Let's go to Hammond's and look around," she said. Hammond's was the biggest department store in the mall. We started down the plaza.

"Did you know Flip invited Ricky Barnes to her party?" Lisa said to Janet. Janet gasped.

"You're kidding! Is he coming?"

"I think so."

"Is Flip having a party?" I asked casually. I hoped my voice didn't give away the pang I felt. Flip and I had spent the whole past month carving up frogs. I would have thought sharing an experience like that should result in an invitation.

At least Janet had the courtesy to look a little apologetic. "Yeah, but it's just for The Club."

"I understand," I said with respect. We were passing a certain boutique, Dazzle, and I paused. "Ooh, look at that." The model in the window was wearing a fabulous long skirt with a sequined top. Everything in the store was sort of wild and gypsyish.

"That stuff's not for you," Janet said decisively. "C'mon, here's Hammond's."

Much as I wanted to go into Dazzle, I liked the

way she was taking charge. And I decided I'd better put myself totally in her hands. I followed them into the department store.

"Look, there's a sale." Lisa pointed at a sign just inside the store's entrance. It read, All Sale Items Are Final.

I knew what that meant. No returns. And a surge of excitement went through me. This was great. If I bought my clothes here, there was no way my mother could take them back. Of course, she'd have a fit when she found out, but by then it would be too late. And I could always fake total innocence and tell her I hadn't seen the sign.

We went to the back of the store, the junior department. I watched as Janet went directly to a rack and started flipping through the clothes. She'd assess each item with a brief look, then thrust it aside. Finally, she pulled out a skirt and sweater combination.

Lisa made a face. "I don't like that."

"Well, it's not for you," Janet said briskly. "This would be good for Mindy."

I wanted to hug her. She was wonderful. I barely glanced at the outfit, but I checked the ticket hanging from it. It said, Half Off, Final Sale. That was all I needed to know.

"This is a great sale," Janet commented as she went to a table of shirts. She pulled one out, held it against the skirt, shook her head, and returned it. She moved on to another rack, and I followed her.

"This is cute," Lisa said, holding up a short red skirt. I nodded eagerly, but Janet dismissed it with a wave of her hand.

"Not for Mindy. Here, hold this."

I accepted the dress she thrust at me. Then she pulled a few more things out. She looked like she knew exactly what she was doing. "You like this, Mindy?"

I wasn't looking at the clothes, I was looking at her. She had such confidence, such assurance. Maybe when I got into The Club, I'd be like that, too.

"Yeah, it's neat."

"C'mon, let's see how all this looks on you." We headed for the dressing rooms. Once inside, she pointed me toward a cubicle. "Try this first."

I pulled off my jeans and T-shirt, and slipped into the skirt and sweater. Then I came out.

"What do you think?" Janet asked Lisa.

"Too tight."

"Yeah. Try on the green, Mindy."

I returned to the cubicle and changed. Then I went back out. "It fits," Lisa said.

Janet approached me, and began adjusting the sleeves. Then she stepped back, and cocked her head to one side. "Turn around," she ordered. I obeyed. As I did, I caught a glimpse of myself in the big wall mirror. My reflection didn't excite me at all.

But Janet was nodding. "That's really nice. It's a definite buy."

"Are you sure?" I asked. I didn't want to argue with her. She probably knew best.

"Absolutely," she said with an authority that washed away any doubts I might have. "Now try the navy dress."

Back in the dressing room, I strained to hear what they were saying. They were talking about Flip's upcoming party Saturday night. What would I be doing on Saturday night? Probably watching television and baby-sitting Valerie. Maybe Peggy could come over and we'd get a video. I tried not to let the thought depress me. Look how well you're getting along with Janet and Lisa, I told myself. Why, in just a few weeks, you'll be going to those parties, too.

Over the next half hour, I must have changed clothes a hundred times. Each time I came out, I avoided the mirror. Instead, I relied totally on their reactions. When I'd finished trying the stuff on that we'd brought in, Janet went out for more.

"Do you think this is me?" I asked Lisa anxiously, fingering the light wool skirt. It was so—brown.

Lisa shrugged. "It's hard to say. I mean, I don't really know you all that well."

She had a point.

"I wouldn't wear it," Lisa continued. "But I'm not you, right?"

Another good point. Janet returned with more clothes. "Look at this."

I did. "Um, I'm not too crazy about brown."

"It's great with your hair," Janet said. "And try this with it." She handed me a beige flannel shirt.

I hate beige. It's the most nothing color in the world. But before I could say anything, Janet gently pushed me back in the cubicle.

By the time we went through all the clothes, I was exhausted. If I had to zip one more zipper or button one more button, I'd scream. Janet had organized the clothes in three piles—the no ways, the maybes, and the absolutely perfects. She asked me exactly how much money I had, then did some rapid calculations.

Then she placed a bunch of things in my arms. "Two skirts, one dress, three shirts, and a sweater. Fantastic!" She looked very pleased with herself.

"Hey, I'm starving," Lisa announced.

"Me too," Janet agreed. "Let's get something to eat." Clutching my clothes, I followed them out of the dressing room. They waited while I paid and got my bags, and we left the store.

I had barely enough money left for a taco, and I couldn't even get a soda, but I didn't care. I was on a high. Any lingering doubts had disappeared. Here I was, sitting with two of the most popular girls at Fox Haven Middle, with a bag of absolutely perfect clothes that my mother couldn't return.

But when Janet and Lisa started discussing what they were wearing Saturday night, I started thinking about my mother's reaction when she found out nothing I'd bought could be returned. Of course, I might be able to convince her that I wasn't aware of the no return policy, but . . .

Something must have shown in my expression, because Janet suddenly asked, "What's the matter?"

"Huh? Oh, nothing." I couldn't tell her. I just had a feeling neither of them would understand. They might even laugh at me. After all, most normal kids can lie to their parents, and their major concern is whether or not they can get away with it. It's only the insecure jerks like me who actually feel bad.

"We better get going," Lisa said to Janet. "Mom's supposed to pick us up in five minutes. She'll drop us at Gayle's."

"We've got a Club meeting," Janet explained to me. I smiled brightly. I hoped they'd tell the others who they'd been with.

"I guess I'd better call my mother," I said. I saw a pay phone in the restaurant, but I didn't get up. I wanted to put off facing her as long as possible.

"Maybe we can drop you off," Lisa said. "Where do you live?"

I told her, and it turned out to be on the way to Gayle's. That put off my confrontation for a little while. And I was hoping maybe my mother wouldn't be home.

But when Lisa's mother pulled up in front of my house, I could see her car in the driveway. "I'll see you guys tomorrow," I said as I got out and thanked Lisa's mother for the ride.

"Wear one of your new outfits," Janet called out the window as they drove away.

"I will," I yelled back. Unless, of course, my mother decided to stuff them in the garbage. And me along with them. Slowly, I dragged myself up the driveway and went in the back door.

Mom was putting dishes in the dishwasher. "Hi," I said. "Need some help?" I dropped my bag, and grabbed a dish.

Not a good move. She immediately knew something was up. She eyed my bag, looking like she was expecting something to jump out of it and bite her. "Okay, let's see what you got."

There was no use trying to put off the inevitable. I sat down at the kitchen table, and she picked up the bag. I closed my eyes. I didn't want to see her face as she examined my purchases. She was probably already prepared to hate it all.

I could hear the tissue paper in the bag crumpling as she drew out the clothes. I waited for a sigh—maybe even a groan. When I didn't hear anything, I opened my eyes.

She was smiling. My mother was actually smiling and nodding as she examined clothes *I* had bought. What was going on here? Had aliens landed and taken over her body?

"*Very* nice," she said. "Oh, I like this! Mindy, I'm pleasantly surprised!"

I was stunned. I stared at her, speechless.

"I'm dying to see this on you! Go upstairs and put it on."

Still in a state of shock, I took the bag and went up to my room. I took out the clothes, and laid them on my bed.

It was as if I was seeing them all for the first time. Suddenly I understood why she liked my clothes. They were exactly what she would have bought.

And I realized something else. I was looking at a pile of the most boring clothes I'd ever seen. I hated them. They weren't me at all. And for once, I couldn't blame my mother.

I couldn't blame Janet either. After all, she didn't force me to get these clothes. And I should have known she'd pick out things that *she* would like. How could I expect her to know my style when I didn't even know what it was?

Boy, had I been stupid. And the tags hanging from the clothes confirmed this.

All sales final. No returns.

I was stuck with these clothes.

Chapter 4

For the sin which we have committed before Thee
by association with impurity . . .

I despise Mr. Murray," Dani announced. "I'd
give him a *minus* ten." We were sitting around the
cafeteria table and rating our teachers on a scale from
one to ten.

"He's pretty creepy looking," I said. Dani gave
me a sidelong look which suggested that she didn't
consider that a particularly brilliant statement.

"I wasn't referring to his looks."

"He's boring, too," I added quickly. Once again,
Dani dismissed me with her eyes, before directing her
remarks to the others.

"He gives pop quizzes. Without any warning at
all! Can you believe it?"

Janet grinned. "That's the whole point of pop
quizzes. If he told you about them ahead of time,
they'd be regular tests."

"We're getting one back today." Dani made a face. "And I'm sure he flunked me again."

"I have him second period," Kelly said. "Actually, those quizzes aren't that hard. The questions are straight out of the textbook."

I nodded. "Yeah, that's why I try to keep up with the assignments."

This time, the look Dani gave me wasn't so subtle. It was downright hostile. "You would." Then she got up. "I'm going to go fix my hair." As she left the table, my eyes followed her for a minute before I turned to the others.

"Why doesn't she like me?"

Lisa's expression was sympathetic. "Don't take it personally."

I raised my eyebrows. "Why not? Are you saying she doesn't like anyone?"

"It's not that, exactly," Lisa said. "It's just that Dani's sort of—"

Gayle interrupted her. "Lisa!"

Lisa clapped a hand over her own mouth. "Sorry." She explained. "It's a rule of The Club. We're not allowed to gossip about each other."

"Lisa!" Gayle and Janet yelled.

"Oops! Sorry again."

Kelly and I avoided each other's eyes. It was times like this that still made me feel like an outsider, and I was sure Kelly felt the same.

When lunch was over, I headed for social studies and the infamous Mr. Murray. I wasn't worried about getting the quiz back. I'd been making straight A's in that class.

Actually, I didn't mind social studies at all. It was an excellent time for daydreaming. Mr. Murray lectured directly from the textbook, so you didn't really have to take any notes. I could tell from my classmates' glazed expressions that no one was listening to him. Occasionally, he'd call on someone to answer a question, and no one knew what the question was. But all you had to say was that you hadn't heard him, and could he please repeat it. Mr. Murray must have thought he had an awfully soft voice because he always believed us. Either that or he assumed half the class had a hearing impairment.

So I sat back in my seat, opened a notebook that contained more doodling than notes, and took out a pen. When Mr. Murray walked in, wearing his usual baggy plaid pants and the striped shirt that clashed, I turned around and grinned knowingly at Dani, sitting three rows behind me. She didn't smile back.

So I turned back toward the front and drifted off into my own private world while old Murray started droning on about South American exports.

I'd been at Fox Haven Middle for three months and some of The Club girls were close to being real friends. Lisa and I had started having a few phone conversations. Flip and I got pretty silly together in biology. Janet was nice. Every time I wore one of those blah outfits I bought with her she made a point of saying how good I looked. I didn't know Marsha or Gayle very well, but at least they weren't snotty.

The only one who acted as if she didn't like me at all was Dani. And that bothered me, because Dani was obviously the leader of them all. I could tell from the way everyone else stopped talking when she opened her mouth. And from the way they all looked especially happy when she complimented them. Or nervous when she criticized them.

She hardly ever spoke to me at all. In fact, she acted like I wasn't even around. The fact that she behaved the same way toward Kelly didn't make me feel any better. I knew if I was ever going to get into The Club, I had to get her to like me.

I tried, I really tried. I told her how much I liked her hair, her clothes, her jewelry, you name it. Sometimes, she'd mumble "yeah, thanks," but most of the time she just looked at me blankly like she didn't care what I thought of her.

We got our quizzes back just before the bell. I checked to make sure I'd received my usual A, and then headed for the door. To my surprise, Dani was waiting for me.

"What did you get?" she demanded.

For a second, I was too stunned to reply. Just hearing a direct question from her had rendered me speechless. When I found my voice, I croaked, "A."

Dani sniffed. "Let me see."

I handed her my test paper. She focused on the grade first, her mouth set in a tight line. Then she looked over the answers. "How did you know the capital of Ecuador?"

"It was in the textbook," I replied.

Dani rolled her eyes. "Oh. And like you said, you read the assignment every night, right?" With that, she whirled around and walked away. I followed her dumbly. We had the same class next—English. But she obviously was not interested in walking with me.

I tried to put all of this out of my mind when I took my seat in English. I liked my English class. I had a great teacher, Ms. Rosen, and we were doing *Romeo and Juliet*. Talk about material for fantasies. But I never daydreamed in English. It was a very involving class. Ms. Rosen was constantly asking us to read aloud and interpret.

Usually, by the end of the class, my arm ached from waving it in the air. This time, however, I was careful not to volunteer too much. I didn't want to show off with Dani in the class.

But if I was surprised after social studies, I was totally shocked to find Dani waiting for me after English. And not just waiting. She was smiling. At me.

"Where are you going now?" she asked.

"Uh, science. In the lab."

"I'm going that way," Dani said. And she started down the hall with me. For a few seconds, we walked in silence. I looked at her. What color were her eyes today—violet? Probably, since she was wearing a long lavender sweater with a matching miniskirt, stockings with lavender dots, and tiny amethyst studs in her ears.

Dani broke the silence. "Do you usually make A's on those social studies quizzes?"

I hesitated. Should I admit I'd never made less? I compromised. "Sometimes." Quickly, I offered an explanation. "You see, I have this really good memory. I mean, I don't have to work very hard. Like, I can remember every word to songs on the radio."

I was floored when Dani actually looked impressed. "Wow, you're lucky. I have a terrible memory."

I smiled uncertainly. "That's too bad."

"Even when I read the assignment, it just goes right out of my head. Poof!" She laughed. "I'm such a dingbat."

I faltered, then I giggled.

"You know," Dani continued, "if I make another F on the next quiz, they'll send a note home to my parents. And do you know what that means?"

I shook my head. She drew a finger across her neck. "They'll *kill* me. I'll be grounded for ages. I'm supposed to be having a sleep-over party in two weeks, and they'll make me cancel it."

"That's awful!" A sleep-over party. Back in Riverside, we called them pajama parties. What I would give to be asked to Dani Dixon's sleep-over! Realistically, I knew I had about as much chance of being invited to the next royal wedding.

When Dani nodded, I thought she was a mind reader. Then I realized she was agreeing with my comment. "No kidding." Then she changed the subject. "You know, the one good thing about social studies is that Murray lets us sit anywhere we like."

"Yeah, that's strange, isn't it? In all my other classes we have assigned seats."

Dani eyed me thoughtfully. "I was just thinking . . . maybe we could start sitting together."

This was too much. Something was going on here.

And her next words confirmed my suspicions. "That way, the next time we have a quiz, I could see your paper."

I gulped. "You mean, you want to copy my answers?"

"Only if I don't know them myself," Dani assured me. "You wouldn't mind, would you?"

I didn't know what to say. And then a loud ringing permeated my cloudy head. "I'm going to be late," I said in a rush. "We'll talk about it later, okay?" And I ran into the science lab.

I was desperate to talk about this, but I didn't mention Dani's idea to Flip in class. Mainly because she probably wouldn't understand the problem. Flip wasn't the type who worried about rules. She'd say something like, "What's the big deal?" Club girls probably all helped each other out like this. I was sure their loyalty to each other was considered more important than—cheating.

I'd never cheated in my life, not in school or anywhere else. Once, when I was buying a candy bar, I was given more change than I was supposed to get. I didn't notice the mistake until I was half a block away from the store. I went back and gave the salesclerk the money.

Of course, this was different. *I* wouldn't be cheating. If Dani wanted to copy from my paper, that was her business. If she got caught, I wouldn't be blamed. Besides, whenever we had quizzes, Mr. Murray sat at his desk and read a book. He wouldn't notice if kids were making paper airplanes out of their quizzes and flying them across the room.

Even so . . . I kept thinking about the code.

Everyone got a copy of it in homeroom the very first day. It was called the Fox Haven Middle School Honor Code. And it didn't just make you promise not to cheat. It said you were supposed to report anyone you observed cheating.

And I'd signed it. I had sworn on my honor to do what the code said. And according to that code, if I knew that Dani was copying from my paper, I was supposed to turn her in.

Well, I certainly couldn't do that. It would mean the end of any chance I might have of getting into The

Club. Not only that, the word would get around, and I'd be shunned by the entire student body. But if I didn't report her, I'd be breaking a solemn oath.

What a mess. But maybe I was worrying unnecessarily. Maybe Dani would forget all about this. After all, she herself told me she had a terrible memory.

"Mindy, would you like my brownie?" Dani's voice at the lunch table contained more sugar than the chocolate square she was offering me.

"No thanks," I replied. "I'm on a diet."

Dani's eyes widened. "Oh, Mindy, you don't need to be on a diet. You've got a cute figure."

I smiled nervously. "Not cute enough." Dani laughed as if I'd just said something hysterically funny. Then she got up. "I better get to class. Are you coming, Mindy?"

"Oh, sure," I said, trying to sound like we walked together to class every day. As we walked, she kept up a steady stream of conversation. "Did you hear they're opening an ice-skating rink where the old bowling alley was? Isn't that neat!"

"Yeah," I replied. "It's neat."

"Do you ice-skate?"

"A little."

"Great!" Her enthusiasm was overwhelming. "Maybe we can all go when it opens." We walked into the classroom. "Let's sit here," she suggested, pointing to a couple of seats toward the back. My stomach turned over. At that very moment, I should have said I'd rather sit up front. But I didn't. I followed her to the back.

There was no pop quiz that day. Mr. Murray's monologue had something to do with the geography of Peru, which I'd read about the night before. This time, however, I didn't have a chance to daydream. Dani kept whispering comments to me about Murray and other kids in the class. It was all I could do to keep from laughing out loud.

For the first time, I understood why she was so admired. A lot of her cracks were kind of mean, cutting people down, making fun of them. But at the same time, they were really funny. And she had a way of making me feel special, like I was the only person in the world she would share her observations with. At one point, I saw a girl turn and look at me enviously. Dani Dixon, the most popular girl in school, was whispering to me.

We walked together to our next class. "It's too bad we can't sit together in English," she said. Her tone was so regretful, I almost believed her. We had just reached the room, when she beckoned me toward the wall and away from the crowd.

"Listen, remember that sleep-over I told you about? Well, it was supposed to be just for Club members, but I think I can talk my parents into letting me have a few more. Would you like to come?"

Somehow, I managed to choke out, "Sure. Love to."

For the rest of the day, visions of pillow fights and midnight pizzas and intimate secret conversations danced in my head. It wasn't until that evening, after dinner, alone in my bedroom with homework stacked in front of me, that I had an attack of the guilts.

That stupid code. What did it mean, anyway? Kids could have been cheating from me before and I never noticed. It was just a piece of paper they made us sign. Probably no one else at school had even bothered to read it.

Besides, I could make sure I didn't actually *see* Dani copy from my quiz. Even though I'd know she was cheating, if I didn't observe it, I wouldn't be obligated to report it.

It was a great rationalization. Too bad it didn't make me feel any better.

I opened my social studies book to the day's assignment, but I couldn't concentrate well enough to read. With all my problems, I just couldn't drum up any interest or concern for the Andean mountains.

I slammed the book shut. I'd do it later. Restlessly, I paced the room. I needed a distraction. I saw my parents setting up a Scrabble board in the dining room. I wandered in.

"Want to play?" my father asked.

My mother blinked when I said okay. She probably couldn't remember the last time I'd agreed to play a board game with them. Neither could I.

"No homework tonight?" she asked.

"Finished it," I lied, sitting down at the table. I gathered my seven blocks and arranged them on the little stand.

The game wasn't as distracting as I'd hoped. My parents were serious Scrabble fanatics and spent ages examining their letter blocks before forming words. While they pondered their letters, I pondered my dilemma.

By the time we finished the game, it was after ten. All my anxieties had taken their toll. I was exhausted and went straight to bed.

The next day, at lunch, Dani talked about her sleep-over party. "My parents just got a wide-screen TV. So we're going to check out tons of videos for my sleep-over. It'll be great!"

There was a general chorus of agreement.

"I was just going to order pizzas," Dani went on. "But then I had a better idea. We're going to have do-it-yourself tacos! We'll have all the stuff laid out, and everyone can make their own. Mindy, what do you think of that?"

"Sounds great."

Once again, we walked to class together and sat together. Mr. Murray walked in. He was carrying a stack of papers. "Pop quiz," he announced.

The usual groan went through the room. I didn't groan, because I was afraid it would emerge from my mouth as a scream. The one night I didn't read the assignment, and we were going to have a quiz.

I knew one lousy F after all my A's wasn't going to really pull down my average. In fact, Mr. Murray had told us at the beginning of the term that he'd drop our lowest pop quiz grade when he averaged the final grades.

So it wasn't for myself that a cold fear enveloped my body. Out of the corner of my eye, I could see Dani's expression. She didn't look bothered by the prospect of a quiz at all. And I knew why.

If only there was some way I could warn her. Whisper "don't copy from me, I didn't do the homework"? Pass her a note? But there was no way. We were right up front, right under Murray's eyes. And as spaced-out as he was, there was no way he could miss any form of communication.

When I got my quiz, I gazed at the questions in horror. Words and phrases jumped out at me. Agricultural products. Exported minerals. The equator.

I looked at Dani, hoping my expression might tell her I didn't know the answers. But she was busily writing her name on the top of the paper.

"Eyes forward," Mr. Murray barked. He took his place at the desk and opened a book. Except for the scratching of pencils, the room fell silent.

I tried to stay calm as I reread the questions. Some of them were multiple choice, so I had a chance. Slowly, I started to write. I had no idea whether or not Dani was copying from my paper.

When the bell rang, I didn't wait for Dani. I dropped my quiz on Murray's desk and fled.

I managed to avoid Dani the rest of the day. And the next morning as well. I even skipped lunch and hid in the library. I considered cutting social studies and going to the infirmary, but how long could I fake sick? Sooner or later I was going to have to face Dani. I might as well get it over with.

Dani was sitting in the back with Marsha again. I guess she figured there was no point sitting next to me today. Murray never gave pop quizzes two days in a row.

When he handed back the tests, I didn't even hold my breath when I turned to the grade. I knew what I'd see, and there it was, one big red letter—F.

At the first note of the bell, I was out of there.

"Mindy!"

Dani's voice was like a bullet, stopping me dead in my tracks. If her voice hadn't done it, her face would have. Her eyes—green this time—were blazing. Her lips were pressed together tightly. And the red in her cheeks didn't come from an abundance of blusher.

"I thought you always got A's."

"I'm sorry," I said miserably. "I didn't do the reading."

She held her quiz in front of my face. "See what I got?"

I blinked. Her big red letter was a C. "But—I got an F!"

"Yeah, well, lucky for me, I didn't copy *all* your answers. I was afraid Murray would get suspicious." Her tone was indignant. "But I assumed I'd get at least a B plus. That's what I needed to get my average up from a D."

"I'm sorry," I said again, but the words sounded hollow.

Dani shoved the quiz in her notebook. "Forget it," she hissed and marched away.

Woefully, I looked after her. Well, at least she wouldn't be copying from me anymore, and I wouldn't be breaking the honor code again.

But she wouldn't be sitting with me again either. And I had a pretty good feeling that her "forget it" didn't just refer to the quiz. I was reasonably certain it included her sleep-over as well.

Chapter 5

For the sin which we have committed before Thee by bribery . . .

What a hunk," Lisa sighed.

Along with Gayle and Janet, I admired the poster advertising the movie currently showing at the theater. Flip moved closer, kissed her fingertips, and pressed them against the lips of the star.

"I wish I could meet a guy like that," Gayle said. "An older guy. *He'd* cheer me up."

"Yeah," Janet agreed. "I hate the week after New Year's. It's such a letdown after the holidays. Nothing to look forward to. No Christmas, no parties—"

"And we go back to school on Monday," Flip finished. "Wow, now I'm really depressed."

"Yeah, me too," I chimed in. That wasn't exactly true. I was probably the only one who was looking forward to school starting up. As far as I was concerned, it was the holiday break that was depressing. Being Jewish, I hadn't had Christmas. As for parties, forget it. I knew Dani had given a New Year's Eve party, but it was strictly for The Club girls. I spent New Year's Eve with Peggy, watching four movie videos in a row. It wasn't awful. At least with Peggy I could relax and not worry about everything I said or did. On the other hand, all evening long I pictured The Club girls doing much cooler things than I was doing.

Gayle was still studying the movie poster. "Want to go see this tonight?"

I waited before responding. Was this a Club thing?

Janet nodded. "Yeah, I'll go."

"Okay with me," Flip said.

I took a chance. "Me too." And no one objected.

What a relief. I wished that spring would hurry up and come, so they could have their rush party. Once I was in The Club, I wouldn't have to feel so insecure about everything.

"I'm going to the movies tonight with some friends," I announced when I got home.

My mother sighed. "Oh, Mindy, I *told* you about tonight. Remember? Your father and I are going to a wedding in New Jersey, and we'll be staying overnight there. You said you'd stay home with Valerie."

"But that was because I didn't think I'd be doing anything else!"

"I'm sorry, honey. But it's too late to get a baby-sitter."

I had to admit she did look sorry. But that didn't

make me feel any better. Here I actually had a chance to do something fun on a Saturday night, and I had to stay home with the geek-in-training. It was too infuriating for words.

As my mother left the kitchen, I scowled at her back. Then I picked up the phone and dialed Flip's number.

"I can't go tonight. My parents are going out of town and I have to stay with Valerie."

I expected to hear something like "too bad," but there was silence on the other end. "Flip? Are you there?"

"Mmm. I was just thinking. They're going to be away overnight?"

"Yeah. Why?"

"Mindy, you could have a party!"

"A party?"

"Yeah! Wait a minute, I want to close the door." When she returned, her voice was hushed, but there was an unmistakable undertone of excitement. "You could have everyone over, and we could party all night!"

By everyone I assumed she meant The Club. I shivered. I couldn't exactly confess that I'd never had a party before. I didn't count those little birthday parties when I was a kid.

"C'mon, Mindy," Flip coaxed. "We do it all the time, whenever anyone's parents go out of town."

"But what if my parents found out? You have no

idea what kind of trouble I'd be in!" I couldn't even begin to guess myself. It was beyond my imagination.

"They'll never find out," Flip assured me. "We'll clean up after ourselves and we'll all be gone by the time they get back."

"You're forgetting someone," I said. "Valerie. She'll tell. She'll probably put an announcement on a banner and hang it from her window."

"Can't you threaten her with something?" Flip asked. "No, wait, I've got a better idea. We'll include her! We'll let her hang out with us!"

Now *that* was an idea. Valerie was always bugging me to let her come with me to the mall on Saturdays. She was dying to hang out with me and my friends. And if she was a willing participant, she couldn't tell on me.

"You won't even have to worry about food and drinks," Flip added. "I'll tell everyone to bring stuff."

It sounded so easy. "Well, . . . okay."

"Great! I'll spread the word. What time are your parents leaving?"

"I'm sure they'll be out of here by eight."

"Okay, see you then!"

Just as I was replacing the receiver, my mother walked in. "Mindy, your father and I have been talking. We've decided it's not really fair of us to make you sit with Valerie all the time."

I looked at her in alarm. "You're hiring a baby-sitter?"

"In a way. We think you should get paid for staying home with your sister. How does twenty dollars sound?"

My mouth fell open. "Uh, great!"

She smiled. "Well, you deserve it. I know you had to give up being with your friends tonight, and I want to make it up to you."

I wished she hadn't said that.

I spent the rest of the day cleaning up my room. I was in the process of dusting my dresser when Valerie materialized.

"Whatcha doing?"

"None of your business."

But it didn't take much for her to figure it out. And leave it to Valerie to get suspicious. I guess I couldn't blame her. This wasn't something I did very often.

But that didn't give her an excuse to start screaming, "Mom, come look! Mindy's cleaning her room!"

Luckily, my parents were running late, and Valerie's announcement didn't have the impact it might have had otherwise. They emerged from their room all dolled up. "We're leaving," my father said. "Now, Val, behave yourself and don't give Mindy any trouble."

"Huh," Valerie snorted. "Why don't you tell her not to give me any trouble?"

My mother fumbled in her purse and pulled out a crisp twenty-dollar bill. "And Mindy, here's your payment in advance."

"Thanks," I said, and stuffed the bill in my jewelry box. Valerie and I followed them downstairs and went through the usual ritual of phone numbers and what-to-do-ifs. Finally, they were gone. Valerie went down to the den and turned on the television. Now I could get ready for my party.

I had spotted a container of sour cream in the refrigerator, and there was a pack of dry onion soup in the cupboard. I was mixing them together when Valerie sauntered into the kitchen. "There's nothing on TV," she whined. "Whatcha doing?"

For once, I didn't respond with my usual "none of your business." Instead, I stopped working and smiled at her. She stepped back in alarm.

"Val, some of my girlfriends are coming over," I began, but she stopped me right there.

"Did you ask Mom and Dad?" she demanded to know. When I shook my head, she beamed.

"I'm telling."

I sat down at the kitchen table and motioned for her to join me. She approached cautiously.

"Val, if I had told them, Mom would have made a fuss and started calling their parents and all that." I winked, like we were sharing a secret. "You know what I mean."

"But you're not supposed to have company without permission," she said. I resisted the urge to strangle her.

"Val, it's no big deal. They're bringing movies and food and we'll just hang out. It'll be fun."

"Fun for *you*," Valerie stated.

"And for you, too," I said quickly. "Don't you want to watch movies with us?"

Valerie stared at me, as if she wasn't sure she had heard correctly. "You mean . . . you're going to let me hang around with you guys?"

I nodded.

Doubt and suspicion crossed her face. But I could see that a struggle was going on. She could hang out with us and pretend she wasn't an obnoxious whiny brat. Or she could tell and get the satisfaction of seeing me in serious trouble. Which would give her the most pleasure?

She made her choice. "Okay."

"Great! Pour these chips in a bowl."

She was still looking dazed as she ripped open the bag. Chips poured out—not in the bowl, all over the floor. It took enormous effort not to start screaming at her.

Flip, Lisa, and Janet arrived first. "I got these," Flip said, handing me a stack of videos.

"Wow," I said. "*Teen Queens in Malibu, High School Zombies*—fantastic!"

Lisa was lugging a humongous makeup case. She opened it to reveal a zillion varieties of eye shadow, blusher, and other stuff. "My mother works for a cosmetics company," she explained. "We can do make-overs."

Janet had brought a big tin of homemade chocolate chip cookies, which Valerie immediately attacked.

"You must be Valerie," Flip said sweetly. "Guys, this is Mindy's sister."

They all responded nicely. Flip had obviously warned them about her. Val's beady eyes searched each face.

"Mindy says I can watch movies with you." She issued that as a challenge. When no one took her up on it, she took another cookie.

Kelly arrived next, and Marsha and Gayle followed soon after. We got to work making a huge batch of popcorn. Then, with a couple of six-packs of sodas, we settled in the den. We allowed Valerie to pick the first movie, and while she pondered her selection, Lisa opened the makeup kit.

"Who wants the first make-over?"

"Me," Janet announced. "And I want to look wild! Everything purple."

"Is Dani coming?" I asked.

"Yeah," Gayle said. "She's with Jason, and he's dropping her off."

"Who's Jason?" I asked.

The Club girls exchanged looks. Only Kelly and I seemed to be ignorant.

"I guess it's okay to tell," Marsha said.

"He's her secret boyfriend," Flip reported. "She has to sneak around to see him."

"How come?" I wondered out loud. And then something Gayle had said clicked. He was dropping her off. "Because he's older? Wow, he *must* be if he can drive."

"Actually, he only has a learner's permit," Flip said. "He's not supposed to drive without an adult in the car, but whenever his parents are out, he takes their car."

"That's dangerous!" I exclaimed. "If the police catch him, he could get into real trouble!"

"That's what I told Dani," Marsha said. "But she doesn't care. You know how Dani is."

I didn't, but I nodded anyway.

"And besides, he's really cute," Lisa added as she stroked purple eye shadow on Janet's lids.

By now, Valerie had stuck a tape into the VCR and a movie had started. I didn't pay much attention to it. I was having too good a time just sitting around and talking. I couldn't believe this was really happening. Here were the most popular girls at school hanging out in *my* den. I glanced at Kelly. She looked extremely happy, too. Briefly, I wondered if The Club had ever gathered at *her* house.

So far so good. Valerie wasn't bothering us. She was hypnotized by the TV screen. And she was beginning to resemble one of the zombies in the movie, with the same glazed-over expression.

"Okay, you guys, look!" Lisa announced. "The new Janet!"

We all started giggling. Lisa had turned preppy Janet into a punk, with purple streaks extending from her eyes almost to her ears. Janet pulled a mirror out of her purse. The look on her face when she saw her reflection turned our giggles into shrieks. We were laughing so hard, I barely heard the doorbell.

"That must be Dani," Flip said, and I dashed upstairs to open the door.

It was Dani, but she wasn't alone. A tall boy with stringy blond hair hanging to his shoulders stood there, too. He had one arm draped around Dani's shoulder and the other encircling a large paper sack.

"Heard you got a party going on," he said. And without another word, he and Dani brushed past me and headed toward the noise in the den.

I followed right behind them. From the expressions on the other girls' faces, I could tell they were just as surprised to see Jason here as I was. We watched the couple in awe, and I marveled at Jason's lack of self-consciousness. Here he was the only boy in a room full of girls, and he didn't seem the least bit uncomfortable. Valerie's eyes drifted toward them for a moment, but then she must have decided the zombies were more interesting.

Jason and Dani flopped down on the sofa, and

Jason put his booted feet on the glass coffee table. I couldn't help wincing when I imagined what my mother would say if she saw that. But that was nothing compared to what both my parents would say if they saw what happened next. Jason opened his paper bag.

"Anyone want a beer?"

That question broke Valerie's trance. She turned completely around and gaped at the sight of Jason popping the top of his can. I shot her a warning look. "Would you like a glass?" I asked Jason, like a good hostess.

"Nah," Jason said. He put the can to his lips and swallowed several times. Then he handed it to Dani, who took a delicate sip.

Flip watched them for a second. "I'll have one."

"Me too," Kelly said quickly.

"Jason, what are you doing here?" Janet asked. "This is an all girls party."

"Not for long," Jason replied.

"What's that supposed to mean?" Lisa asked.

"Some friends of mine are coming over."

It took me a moment to absorb the significance of this. When it hit me, I felt dizzy. Boys. Older boys. Coming here.

Lisa gathered up her makeup. "I'll be right back." Janet and Kelly followed her out. "I'll call and order some pizzas," Gayle announced.

I just stood there for a moment, still in a daze. "Excuse me," I mumbled. I ran upstairs to my room.

It was a mob scene in there. Everyone was jostling for a position in front of the mirror. Janet was frantically rubbing a tissue over her purple eyelids. Lisa was making use of my perfume.

"Mindy, do you have any mousse?" Kelly asked.

"Yeah, in the bathroom. I'll get it." I went across the hall. Catching a glimpse of my own reflection in the bathroom mirror, I decided I could use a little makeup, too. I'd gone strangely pale.

Back in my room, Flip and Marsha had joined the others in the battle for mirror space. "Does anyone know Jason's friends?" I asked.

"No, but I'll bet they're cool," Flip said. "Mindy, you're biting your nails."

I wasn't even aware of that. I clutched my hands together behind my back. My palms were sweating.

"High school boys," Gayle murmured. "Don't worry, Mindy. We'll let you have first pick. After all, it's your party."

I managed a thin smile. High school boys. I could barely speak to boys my own age.

"And it's gonna be a great one," Flip exclaimed with glee. "Mindy, this party's gonna go down in history!"

I caught a glimpse of Kelly eyeing me in the mirror. There was an odd expression on her face. Jealousy. I was one step closer to The Club now than she was. Maybe it was mean of me, but it did give me a little thrill of pleasure.

Lisa giggled. "Boy, if my parents knew I was at a party with high school boys . . ." She drew a finger across her throat.

If my parents knew I was *giving* a party with high school boys—and then, like an unpleasant reminder, I saw Valerie standing in the doorway. With a crooked finger, she beckoned to me. I stepped out into the hall.

"Are boys coming here?"

I tried to sound casual, like boys dropped by here all the time. "Yeah."

Her eyes became narrow slits. "If Mom and Dad ever found out about this—"

"But they won't, right?"

"Can I stay up as late as I want and watch all the movies?"

Did I have a choice? "Sure. Why don't you go back to the den and watch them?"

Valerie made a face. "They keep giving me dirty looks."

I remembered that Dani and Jason were still down there. "I'll go back with you."

Dani and Jason weren't missing us. They were still on the couch, only now they were locked together in each other's arms. When they heard us on the steps, Dani opened her eyes. With a distinct look of annoyance aimed at me, she extracted herself from Jason's arms.

I glanced at the TV. "Is this movie any good?"

Dani's reply was icy. "We weren't exactly watching."

Luckily, all the others started returning. And then the doorbell rang. The girls looked at me expectantly. It was my house. I had to answer the door.

I ran back up the stairs and wiped my palms on my jeans before opening the door. Three guys stood there. I gave them a quick once-over, though nothing really registered, except for the fact that one of them was kind of pimply.

"Hi," one of them said in a voice so deep it made me jump. "Jason here?"

I'd heard of people being tongue-tied but I never knew what it meant until that moment. All I could do was nod, step aside, and point mutely to the stairs leading down to the den. I followed behind them.

Valerie sidled next to me as the hum of conversation grew louder. "That guy's smoking," she whispered.

"Shh," I hissed. "But remind me to spray the room with deodorizer when they leave."

Suddenly, my little party changed dramatically. The addition of these three boys made the room feel crowded. Then someone put an album on the stereo and turned it up full blast. It drowned out the television, and I expected to hear Valerie scream in protest. Instead, she sunk down into her chair and watched the room with her eyes wide and her mouth slightly open.

Lisa automatically paired herself with one of the boys, and Flip with another. The third one took a beer and sat on the couch. With Marsha, Gayle, Janet, and Kelly sitting on the floor at his feet, he looked like a sultan with a harem.

I didn't know where to go or what to do. I wished the pizzas would come so I could busy myself serving them. Then something happened that made all visions of pizza evaporate.

The boy on the couch pulled something out of his pocket and put it on the coffee table. It was a plastic bag. And even though I'd never seen this stuff before in real life, I knew what it was.

I hadn't been too crazy about having beer at my party, but at least beer was legal. I beckoned frantically to Flip, but she was dancing now and didn't see me.

Kelly appeared by my side. "Mindy, he's got pot."

"I know," I replied. "What should I do?"

"Well, you can't exactly tell him to put it away. You'll look like a real geek."

The boy was rolling joints now. Janet joined us. "Are you going to try it?"

"I don't know." Kelly giggled nervously. "I've never smoked pot before."

"Me neither," Janet said.

I'd been chewing voraciously on a fingernail as they talked. A sickeningly sweet smell filled the air. We all watched as the boy sucked in the smoke.

"Why isn't he blowing it out?" I asked.

"You're supposed to keep it in your lungs as long as possible," Janet told us. "That's how you get high."

High. I'd never seen people high on drugs except in the movies. They'd probably all start acting really goofy pretty soon. The boy handed the joint to Jason, who took a drag, and then handed it to Dani. The whole process looked terribly unsanitary.

"I'm going to try it," Kelly announced. I knew she was just trying to impress the others, but, even so, I had to admire the confident way she strode over to Dani and accepted the joint.

She took a short, tentative puff. Then she took a longer one. Suddenly, she started coughing, and her face turned green. "I think I'm going to be sick," she croaked.

Dani eyed her in disgust. I grabbed Kelly's arm and pulled her toward the bathroom. Kelly staggered inside and shut the door.

When I returned, the smell was getting stronger. Several joints were making the rounds now. One of the boys took a beer and shook it before flipping the tab. It sprayed all over the place. The boys started laughing like hyenas. And now I was getting really nervous.

I wasn't alone. Marsha and Gayle came over to me. "Mindy, this is getting weird. Maybe you should do something."

"Like what?" I asked in a panic.

Neither of them had any brilliant suggestions. Across the room I saw Lisa climb up on an end table and start dancing.

Dani sauntered over to us. She offered the joint to Marsha, who shook her head. "I'm allergic." Dani looked at her in disbelief, then extended it to Gayle. Gayle took it gingerly, and barely touched it to her lips. "Honestly, you guys," Dani said, shaking her head. She took the joint back and held it out to me.

I felt sick. Here was a chance to really impress Dani, but I had this awful vision of myself having the same reaction as Kelly. And not making it to the bathroom on time.

Thank goodness, the doorbell rang. "That must be the pizza man," I said. I turned away and went back up to the living room.

But it wasn't the pizza man. It was Peggy. And she looked distinctly uncomfortable. "My parents sent me over to ask you to turn the music down. The neighbors on your other side called them. They wanted to call the police."

"The police!" My head was spinning. I was aware that the odor of the pot had drifted up to the living room and wondered if Peggy could smell it.

"They won't call them," Peggy assured me. "As long as you turn the music down." Raucous laughter drifted up from the den. "Are you having a party?"

"It's not really a party," I said hastily. "Some kids came by and, you know . . ." My voice trailed off. This was the point where I should invite Peggy to join us. But I didn't. I looked at Peggy standing there, in old corduroy pants that were too short and a Snoopy sweatshirt peeking out from under her coat. She just wouldn't fit in. Plus, I knew how shocked she'd be by the beer and the pot and the older boys.

She was gazing with frank curiosity at the stairs that led down to the den. And I felt like scum.

"Where's the pizza?" Lisa stood in the entrance to the den.

"It wasn't the pizza delivery man," I called over my shoulder. "Hey, turn the music down, okay? Or the neighbors are calling the police."

Lisa squinted at the door. "Oh, hi, Peggy."

"Hi," Peggy replied.

"Lisa, *please* turn down the music," I said again. Lisa didn't seem to have heard me. She went out to the kitchen. I turned back to Peggy. "I better go turn it down myself. Listen, Peggy, um, don't tell your parents I had people here, okay? Because my parents are out of town, and I don't want them to find out."

"Okay," Peggy said. "Have fun." And she was gone.

I stared after her for a minute. I knew what she must be feeling. She had to be hurt. But what else could I have done?

I could have invited her to come in and not cared what the others thought. That's what I could have done. Maybe she'd be shocked by the beer and the pot and the older boys—but I should never have let any of them inside in the first place. This wasn't the kind of party I'd wanted to have.

Then I heard a crash. I ran back downstairs. Someone had knocked over a lamp. Shattered pieces were scattered on the floor. A bottle of beer had overturned and was dripping down the coffee table. Two of the boys were competing to see who could drink a bottle of beer faster, and the girls were cheering them on.

And there was Valerie, huddled on the floor. She looked frightened. My little baby sister was scared out of her mind. I couldn't help myself—I cared. I had a crazy urge to envelop her in my arms and comfort her.

I knew what I had to do. First I went to the stereo and turned it down. "What did you do that for?" Flip asked.

"I think everyone better leave," I said. "The neighbors are complaining. And my sister's freaking out."

"But we're having so much fun," Flip protested.

Kelly looked positively stunned. "You're going to throw everyone out?"

"Well, the girls can stay," I compromised.

"Dani's going to hate you," Kelly warned.

I knew that. Then I took one more look at Valerie.

"I don't care," I lied. "It's my house." I had to scream those last words. Someone had turned the stereo back up.

I strode over there and lifted the needle. The sudden silence got everyone's attention. "Mindy, what are you doing?" Dani demanded to know.

I took a deep breath. "I think the guys better leave."

"Why?" Janet asked.

"Because—because I want them to. And it's my party." I winced at how childish that must have sounded. But I could have sworn I saw relief cross the faces of several girls.

Not Dani, though. Her upper lip curled into a sneer. Then, in a bored voice, she said, "Okay, let's all go to my place. My parents are out."

"The girls can stay," I offered weakly.

But they were all gathering their coats. Flip came over and whispered in my ear. "You want me to stay and help you clean up?"

It was nice of her to offer, but her eyes were begging me to say no. "That's okay," I said. "You can go."

Flip smiled gratefully. Glancing furtively at Dani, she hissed, "I don't blame you for kicking them out. I wouldn't want this going on at my party." Then she went to get her coat.

Within seconds, the house was empty. I leaned

against the closed door and breathed easier. Then the bell rang again.

It was the pizza delivery man. "I'm sorry," I said. "You must have the wrong house."

He checked the lid of the pizza box. "But isn't this—"

"No." I closed the door in his face. Then I went back to the den. What a mess. Valerie emerged from her corner, and I was glad to see that the fear had disappeared from her eyes. "I'm sorry," I told her honestly. "I didn't know it would be like this." I put an arm around her and pulled her close.

We stood there for a moment. Poor baby, I thought. Then Valerie pushed my arm off. "I'm going to tell."

"What?"

"I'm going to tell Mom and Dad you had a party, and there were boys, and beer and . . ." she paused, and then added with dramatic emphasis, "drugs."

I couldn't believe it. Because of her I'd just thrown the most popular girls at school out of my house, and this whining, sniveling, rotten child was threatening to tell on me! "Valerie! You can't!"

An all-too-familiar smirk appeared on her face. "Oh yes I can."

Images raced through my mind. No allowance, no phone calls, no television, grounded for the rest of my natural life. There was only one way to save myself.

I began negotiations. "You can have my Madonna T-shirt."

She shook her head.

"My T-shirt and my charm necklace."

Again, she shook her head.

There wasn't much left. "My T-shirt, my necklace, and half the money Mom gave me."

She gazed at me steadily.

"Okay, *all* the money."

That did it. She followed me up to my bedroom. Silently, and with the dirtiest looks I could muster, I handed over the T-shirt, the necklace, and the twenty-dollar bill. Without even a thank-you, she went to her room.

Going back to survey the disaster in the den, I thought it could have been worse. At least I'd stood up for myself. And as I swept up the pieces of broken lamp, I knew I'd done the right thing, making them leave.

And I tried not to think about the fact that I'd be twenty dollars richer if I hadn't let all this happen in the first place.

Chapter 6

*For the sin which we have committed before Thee
by breach of trust . . .*

I was sitting on the concrete front steps of my
house, reading. My rear end was getting sore. Normally, on a Sunday afternoon, I'd be doing this lying
comfortably on my bed. But it was unusually warm
and sunny for March, and my mother had this thing
about making me go outside on nice days.

Peggy's mother's car pulled into the driveway
next door, and I could see Peggy sitting on the pas-
senger side. I hardly ever saw Peggy anymore. We
didn't walk to school together because she'd started
going to the Y early in the morning for a gymnastics
class before school. Besides, ever since the night of my
so-called party, I'd felt uncomfortable around her.

I was surprised to see Peggy's mother go around
to the side and open Peggy's door. And I was shocked
when Peggy emerged clutching a crutch in one arm.

"What happened?" I asked as I approached the
car.

"Bad landing off the beam," Peggy said, wincing as she limped toward their door.

"Torn ligaments," Mrs. Cavanaugh explained. "She'll be fine in a couple of weeks. And the doctor said she probably won't even need the crutch in a few days."

"But I'm off the team for the rest of the season," Peggy said.

Even though I couldn't relate to her passion for gymnastics, I knew this was a major blow. One look at her wan face told me how depressed she was. So when her mother asked me if I wanted to come in and have lunch with them, I quickly agreed, even though I'd already eaten and wanted to get back to my book. Poor Peggy needed cheering up. Maybe this was my chance to make up for not inviting her to my party.

"It's just leftovers," Mrs. Cavanaugh said as I helped Peggy ease into a chair at the kitchen table. "The men of the house are out playing golf."

I knew what "leftovers" in Cavanaugh language meant. And even though I wasn't hungry, I was pleased to see Peggy's mother heating up her fabulous macaroni and cheese.

Peggy carefully set her injured foot on a chair, and eyed it in mournful resignation. "I guess it could have been worse. But what am I going to do all spring if I can't be in gymnastics?"

"You've got other interests," I said, trying to

sound upbeat. "Now you've got more time for them. Like . . . like . . ." I couldn't think of any other interests she had that didn't involve running around.

Peggy sighed. "I don't have any other interests."

"Well, then maybe you should develop some," I suggested.

"Now there's a thought!" Mrs. Cavanaugh said as she placed the casserole dish on the table. Peggy gazed at it in total disinterest. *I* was practically drooling.

Mrs. Cavanaugh joined us at the table and leaned toward me. "Let's think of something we can get Peggy involved in," she said. Something about her conspiratorial tone made me feel very wise and mature.

Peggy poked at her macaroni listlessly while I pondered this. "I think," I began slowly, "that she should get more involved in school activities."

"Excellent idea!" Mrs. Cavanaugh exclaimed. "I've been telling her that for ages! Maybe she'll listen to you."

"Hey, don't talk about me like I'm not here!" Peggy complained. Then she gave us a weak smile. "Sorry."

I patted her shoulder. Peggy just wasn't a natural whiner, like me. She had to be pretty upset to be moaning like this.

"But what kind of school activities?" she asked.

"I'm not into theater stuff, and I don't want to work on the school paper. They wouldn't want me anyway."

She was probably right. The Drama Club and the Middle School Report were pretty closed cliques. I took a bite of macaroni and chewed pensively.

"I've got it!" I said suddenly. "Did you hear that announcement Friday about Deedee Sloane?" I explained to Mrs. Cavanaugh. "Deedee's eighth grade class treasurer, and she's moving away. So there's going to be a special election for a new treasurer. Peggy could run for it."

Since she had good manners, Peggy took a second to finish chewing and swallow before her mouth fell open. "Run for class treasurer?"

"Yeah! You're good in math, and you're very organized. You'd be perfect!"

"That's a wonderful idea!" Mrs. Cavanaugh exclaimed.

Peggy's mouth remained open as her eyes moved from my face to her mother's. "But I don't know anything about running for election."

"*I* do," I said. "I ran for seventh grade secretary back in Riverside." I didn't think it was appropriate to add that I hadn't won. "I can help plan your campaign and come up with slogans and speeches and all that stuff."

"Speeches?" Peggy asked faintly.

But her mother was full of enthusiasm. "This

could be a great opportunity for you, Peggy. Even if you don't win, just think of the fun you'll have, the people you'll meet, the new friends you could make."

"Class treasurer . . ." Peggy murmured. "I don't even know what a treasurer does."

I didn't either. Of course, I knew it had something to do with money, but I had no idea where it came from and what it was spent on. "We'll find out."

Peggy still didn't look convinced. As a final inducement, I said, "There's only four months left in the school year, so if you hate the job it won't be for too long. And if you like it, then next year you can run for treasurer in high school."

"And it will keep you from moping around the house," Mrs. Cavanaugh added.

"Okay, okay," Peggy said. "I mean, I'll *think* about it."

But I knew she'd do it. I could tell from her expression. And I was glad, not just for her, but for myself, too.

It was strange. If anyone treated me the way I'd treated Peggy, I'd hate that person. Peggy was forgiving. At least now I'd have an opportunity to earn her forgiveness.

Special Election for Eighth Grade Treasurer, read the sign just outside my homeroom door. Sign Up Today in the Main Office.

"I'm going to do it."

I turned to see Peggy standing there, leaning on her crutch.

"Great!" I replied.

"And you'll help me with the campaign?"

"Absolutely," I promised.

Peggy studied the sign. "I wonder who else is running."

"I don't know," I said. "Hey, maybe nobody else will run. Then you'll win without even campaigning."

Peggy grinned. "I better not count on that." And she hobbled off in the direction of the office.

She was right. Someone else was running. And I found out who it was at the lunch table.

"I'm going to run for class treasurer," Gayle announced. "I just signed up at the office."

"What do you want to do that for?" Lisa asked.

Dani answered this. "Because then she can say she has experience next year when it's time for ninth grade elections. It's going to be important for us to hold offices in high school."

"Why?" Flip asked.

"So we can have more influence," Dani began, but then she snapped her mouth shut. Kelly and I lowered our heads and acted like we weren't listening.

"Does anyone know what the class treasurer does?" Gayle asked.

"It's something to do with money, that's all I know," Lisa said.

"If that means spending it, you'll be great," Flip noted.

Gayle laughed. "And all you guys are going to help me on the campaign, right?" There was a general bobbing of heads around the table. Mine was one of them.

Peggy called me at home that night. "I'm really glad you talked me into this. I'm actually getting excited."

I was glad she couldn't see my face as I said, "That's good."

"I better start planning my campaign right away. Can we meet tomorrow?"

"Sure. How about after supper?"

"Okay." There was a pause. "You know, I would never have the guts to do something like this if you weren't helping me."

"No problem," I said. "See you tomorrow."

Now what, I wondered as I replaced the receiver. If I didn't campaign for Gayle, I'd never get into The Club. But I'd promised Peggy, and I couldn't go back on my word.

There was only one possible solution. I'd campaign for both. And just make very sure neither of them ever found out.

The announcement of the candidates came over the intercom the next morning in homeroom. "For eighth grade treasurer," the voice intoned, "Peggy Cavanaugh and Gayle Edwards."

Gayle, sitting behind me, whispered in my ear, "Can you come over to my house after school? We're going to plan my campaign."

I nodded. After school—that was good. I didn't have to go to Peggy's till after supper. At least there was no conflict in time. Little matters like homework would just have to wait.

All day, I found it very hard to concentrate in my classes. Questions were buzzing around my brain. Would I really be able to work for both candidates and keep it a secret? What if I had some really super idea for a poster, or a slogan, or something like that—who would I give it to?

If I gave my best ideas to Gayle, it could definitely pay off when The Club chose its new members. On the other hand, Gayle had a whole slew of friends ready and willing to help her. Peggy needed me.

But that afternoon at Gayle's, I soon realized that if I didn't come up with an idea, Gayle wasn't going to have much of a campaign. We were all gathered in her living room, talking about everything but the election. Finally, Gayle brought the subject up.

"When I told my father I was running for treasurer, he flipped," she said, giggling. "He said I can't even handle my own allowance!"

"Did you find out anything about what the treasurer does?" Marsha asked.

"I asked Deedee Sloane," Janet said. "She told me the treasurer is responsible for raising money and making a budget."

"How did she raise money?" Gayle asked.

"She didn't," Janet replied. "There's no money at all in the eighth grade treasury. That's why we're not getting a class trip, like the seventh grade. They're going to New York for a day."

"She doesn't sound like she was a very good treasurer," I commented.

Janet agreed. "She just wanted the title, she didn't want to do any work. She never even had to make a budget because there wasn't any money to put in it!"

"Hey, this sounds like a pretty easy job!" Gayle exclaimed.

"At least you won't have any trouble getting elected," Flip noted. "No one knows Peggy Cavanaugh."

I do, I said silently. But aloud, I said, "You still need to campaign. I think we should make posters with slogans. Something cute and catchy."

Gayle picked up a pen and pad. "Got any ideas?"

I thought about it. "Um, what do you think of 'Trust Your Money with Gayle'? Or how about, 'Cash In with Gayle'?"

The response was less than enthusiastic. "That sounds stupid," Dani stated.

It was on the tip of my tongue to come back with

a snappy "can you think of anything better?" but I restrained myself. There was no point to making a worse enemy of Dani. She disliked me enough already.

"I think the signs should be simple and elegant," Dani continued. "Just 'Gayle Edwards for Eighth Grade Treasurer.'"

I couldn't believe the way everyone in the room greeted that boring suggestion. She really had them all on a string.

"I'll get markers and posters," Gayle said. "We can make the signs tomorrow afternoon and have them up in the halls Thursday morning. What colors should I get?"

While the group debated the merits of black on white over red on yellow, I tried to think of some way to redeem myself. I had to present at least one solid idea. And then I had it.

"You know, people running for office usually put their signs up on the walls in the hallways. Kids walk right past them and don't even read them. I think we should put ours someplace else. Where kids would definitely see them."

"Like where?" Gayle asked.

I beamed. "In the rest room cubicles! In the girls' rooms we'll put them on the inside door. And we can get some guy to put them in the boys' rooms, on the walls, so the boys will have to look at them when they—you know."

I paused, waiting for everyone to acknowledge

my brilliance. The response wasn't exactly what I expected.

"Ooh! Ick!" That came from the vicinity of Kelly and Lisa.

"That's gross!" Janet exclaimed.

And Dani looked at me as if I was some disgusting thing that crawled on the ground.

"Well, I just figured we'd have a captive audience," I said lamely.

At least Flip was grinning. "That's true. But do we really want people to be thinking about Gayle when they're going to the bathroom?"

I saw her point. It was time to change the subject. "Do you know what your platform's going to be?" I asked Gayle.

She looked at me blankly. "My what?"

"Your platform. You know, you have to give a speech at the assembly on Monday and tell the class what you'll do if you're elected."

Gayle seemed totally bewildered. "I don't have the slightest idea what I'm going to do. I thought I'd wait and see if I get elected first. I mean, why should I spend time making plans when I might not even get the job?"

"You'll get it," Dani stated. "Who'd vote for Peggy Cavanaugh anyway?"

"I don't know about that," Lisa remarked. "There are a lot of nerds in this school, and they just might band together."

"I wonder what *her* platform is," Gayle pondered. Lisa turned to me.

"Doesn't she live next door to you?"

I nodded. Lisa clapped her hands. "Hey, maybe you could find out what she's planning! You could pretend you want to help on her campaign, and then tell us what she's going to do."

I gulped. "You mean—spy on her?"

"That's a great idea!" Dani exclaimed. For the first time in ages, she was actually looking at me with something other than disdain in her eyes. "You'd be doing us a big favor, Mindy."

A big favor. Those words had major implications. But spy on Peggy? How could I do that to her?

They were all watching me, waiting for my response. My mind was racing. Of course, I could *say* I'd do it, but not really pass on anything important. And I wouldn't have to worry about any of them finding out I'd been working with Peggy—they'd think I was doing it for them.

"I guess I could do that," I said slowly. For a second, I thought I saw Marsha frown. I couldn't be sure. What I could be sure of was the approval on Gayle's face. More importantly, I saw the same look on Dani's. It made for a nice change.

Cavanaugh Campaign Headquarters had a decidedly different tone than Gayle's. For one thing, the only workers were me, Peggy, and her drippy friend Karen. And the mood was not optimistic.

"I don't think I'll get many votes," Peggy said. "Not that many kids know me."

"You're probably right," Karen agreed.

Her negativity annoyed me. "Then you'll have to make kids know you," I said with as much spirit as I could muster.

"How?" Peggy asked. "And don't tell me I have to stand at the entrance every morning and shake hands. I couldn't do that."

I shook my head. "No, that's not the way. Let me think." I took a second, maybe a third, brownie. I always said chocolate had a tendency to stimulate my imagination.

"How's this? You know how all the clubs meet after school? Maybe you could go around to the meetings and introduce yourself. That way you could meet a whole bunch at once."

Peggy winced. "You mean, speak in front of a whole group?"

"You're not very good at public speaking," Karen noted. I made a face at her, and turned full attention to Peggy.

"There aren't that many kids at those meetings. Besides," I added, "you're going to have to give a speech on Monday. It will be good practice for you." I pulled a copy of the Middle School Report from my bag and turned to the page that listed the extracurricular activities for the week.

"Let's see, tomorrow's Wednesday . . . okay, the Science Club has a meeting, and the Future Teachers do, too. On Thursday there's the French Club, the Spanish Club, and the History Club. And on Thursday morning, the Library Aides have a meeting. All you have to do is show up and ask if you can have one minute to introduce yourself and tell them why you're running."

"Why I'm running . . ." Peggy's forehead puckered. Then she grinned. "Hello, my name is Peggy Cavanaugh, and I'm running for class treasurer because I tore some ligaments and can't do gymnastics and I need something else to do."

"I don't think that's a very good idea," Karen said. I ignored her. The girl had absolutely no sense of humor.

Peggy looked at me plaintively. "What do you think I should tell them?"

I shrugged. "Well, what would you do if you were treasurer?"

Peggy considered this. "I guess," she began slowly, "I'd try to come up with some unusual ways for the class to make some money."

"Like what?" Karen demanded to know.

"A car wash?"

"That's boring," I said. "Look, why don't you say you'll appoint a committee to study fund-raising possibilities? That'll sound good. And then you can talk about what the class could spend the money on."

"I know what I'd say about that," Peggy said. "Books for the library. The librarian told me that the county cut her book budget this year."

I frowned. Books for the library sounded good to me, but what would the majority of students think of that? I doubted they'd find it more appealing than a class trip.

"Well, okay . . . let's talk about signs and slogans."

"No signs," Peggy said unexpectedly. I stared at her.

"You *have* to have signs! Everyone has signs!"

Peggy shook her head firmly. "I just can't stand the thought of walking down the halls and seeing my name all over the place. It gives me the creeps."

"But Peggy, you need people to know your name!"

Obstinately, she shook her head again. "No signs."

"I have an idea," Karen said.

I pretended to be interested, but I could just imagine what kind of idea *she'd* have.

"I'm going to that Library Aides meeting Thursday morning. I could get to school early, and write something about Peggy on the blackboard in all the homerooms."

"The teachers will just erase it when they come in," I objected.

"Yeah, but lots of students get into the homerooms before the teachers do," Karen said. "And they'll see the message before the teacher erases it. And that way, Peggy won't have to see her name all over the place all day."

Actually, in all fairness, I had to admit it wasn't such a terrible idea. I turned to Peggy. "What do you think?"

She made a face. "Well, it's better than signs, I guess. What are you going to write?"

Karen spent several minutes contemplating this. "How about 'Vote Peggy Cavanaugh for Eighth Grade Treasurer'?"

She wasn't any more original than Dani.

"I'm more worried about this speech on Monday," Peggy said.

"I'll help you with it," I promised.

"Saturday?" she asked hopefully. "Oh, I forgot. You go to the mall on Saturdays."

"Maybe I could get back early. Anyway, sometime on Saturday we'll work on it." I looked at my watch and practically screamed. Almost nine o'clock, and I hadn't even started my homework.

We left Karen in the living room as Peggy walked me to the back door. "Listen," she said. "I know you're friends with Gayle Edwards and her crowd. And I want you to know I really appreciate that you're helping me with my campaign even though I'm running against her."

Somehow, I managed to smile.

We sprawled on the floor of Gayle's living room with stencils and markers and big poster boards. I was just in the middle of carefully inking in the word *for* when Dani asked, "Did you find out anything about Peggy's campaign, Mindy?"

My hand slipped, turning the *o* in *for* into a *q*. I reached for the correction fluid. "No, not really. She's just doing the usual stuff."

"Like what?" Dani persisted. "What is she putting on her signs?"

"Actually, she's not making signs."

"She's not?" Heads turned in disbelief. "What's she doing instead?" Gayle asked.

I focused my attention on applying an additional, unnecessary layer of correction fluid to the poster. "Oh, nothing major, really." I made every effort to sound unconcerned, vague, nonchalant. But like my mother always said, I was a lousy actress. And here was the living proof. All eyes in the room were on me. And they were all shining with suspicion.

"Mindy, you know something." Kelly almost sounded like a police officer.

"C'mon, Mindy, tell us," Gayle wheedled.

Reluctantly, I raised my head, and found myself

looking directly into Dani's eyes. I realized that this was it—the big test. Where were my loyalties? Briefly, I saw Peggy's face in my mind—her trusting, grateful face. But it faded as Dani's eyes bored into my head.

It was as if the words left my mouth without my even saying them, like the power of my voice had overcome my mind, and my conscience. "This friend of hers, Karen, she's going to write 'Vote for Peggy' on the homeroom blackboards before school tomorrow."

There was a moment of silence as this sunk in. "That's dumb," Flip said. "The teachers will just erase it."

"Absolutely," I said quickly. "See, I told you it was nothing important."

"But kids will see the message before the teacher erases it," Kelly pointed out.

There was another silence, which Dani broke. "We'll take care of that."

And sure enough, the next morning when I walked into my homeroom, the blackboard was bare. Someone had gotten into the rooms right after Karen. And that someone had erased the blackboards.

We didn't go to the mall Saturday. Instead, we met at Gayle's to help her prepare her speech for Monday. I kept an eye on my watch. I'd told Peggy

I'd be at her place at three. And I wasn't going to let her down.

I could have gotten out of going to Gayle's, claiming I was sick or something. But I needed to be here, to find out what Gayle was planning to say. Because I was going to report it all to Peggy. Even though she didn't know why her message was erased from the blackboards, I had to make it up to her. It was on my conscience.

It turned out that Gayle didn't really need our help. She knew exactly what she was going to say.

"Nobody likes long speeches," she told us. "So all I'm going to say is how we'll get some money and what we're going to spend it on."

We waited in breathless anticipation.

"Now, I don't want to get involved in some stupid fund-raising thing. It takes too much work. So get this. I'm going to have eighth grade dues! Everyone will pay two dollars. There's about ninety kids in the class. That makes—" she stopped.

"One hundred and eighty dollars," someone supplied.

Gayle acknowledged this gratefully. "Thanks. I'm terrible in math."

As those words penetrated my head, I clenched my hands in excitement. This was it. This was what I'd been hoping for.

"And then," Gayle continued, "we'll spend the

money on a real dance! With a band, and decorations, and everything!"

The room burst into applause. Automatically, my hands unclenched and began clapping. But my mind was spinning in a hundred directions.

Everyone was talking, and I edged my way over to Gayle. "Those are neat ideas," I said. "By the way, I'm awful in math, too. I can barely keep a B average."

"I'd be lucky if I could even get a B," Gayle replied. "I always get C's in math."

My mission was accomplished. I had my ammunition. "Listen, I've got to go. I have to do something with my mother."

Gayle didn't even hear me. She was talking with Lisa. But as I went toward the door, I heard a discussion that stopped me.

"Marsha, you know that gold belt you never wear?" Flip was saying. "It would go perfectly with my green sweater dress. Do you want to sell it?"

"Sure," Marsha said. "Five dollars?"

"Okay."

Funny, how some trivial piece of conversation can set off a whole chain of ideas. I practically ran all the way to Peggy's.

I was panting when I came through the door. "I've got a fantastic idea for fund-raising."

"Great!" Peggy exclaimed. "Because I can't think of anything but the same old bake sales and stuff like that. What's your idea?"

"A clothes exchange! Kids bring in all the stuff they never wear or they're sick of. Then we sell it to other kids!"

"That's tremendous!" Peggy squealed. "And we can use the money to buy books for the library!" She gazed at me with unconcealed admiration. "Mindy, you're brilliant!"

I smiled modestly. "And now, I've got some information that could definitely win this election for you." I paused dramatically. "Are you ready?"

Peggy nodded, her eyes wide.

"Gayle Edwards makes C's in math."

It seemed to take a few moments for this to register. And finally, Peggy's expression changed. But instead of looking excited, she actually looked sad.

"That's too bad. She shouldn't be running for treasurer if she's bad in math."

"Exactly! And if you tell everyone that in your speech, they'll never vote for her!"

I waited for a gleam of triumph to appear in her eyes. But it didn't happen. "I couldn't do that."

"Why not?"

"It's dirty politics. I don't want to get involved in name-calling or anything like that."

"But Peggy," I protested, "you could win if people knew Gayle can barely add!"

"I don't want it to be like that. If I win, I want it to be on my own merits."

I wanted to argue with her, but I couldn't. She

wouldn't change her mind anyway. There was one thing I knew for sure about Peggy. She had integrity.

But I had a sinking suspicion integrity wouldn't count for much in a middle school election.

The eighth grade assembly was held on Monday morning. I stayed in the rest room until the very last minute, so I could slip in and sit in the back. I didn't want to sit with Peggy's friend Karen. But I didn't want to sit with The Club girls either.

Peggy went first, and her speech was solid. Even though her voice was a little shaky, she explained her plans well, and she sounded very serious. She'd even worn a dress, and although it wasn't very fashionable, she looked halfway decent.

Gayle, on the other hand, looked great. But she acted a little silly, giggling between every other sentence, and her platform didn't have much substance. It wasn't nearly as logical or intelligent as Peggy's.

Ballots were passed out. I've never before been so grateful to be an American. The secret voting process is a wonderful thing. Without anyone knowing, I was able to vote for the person I knew would make the better treasurer. The ballots were collected, and we were told the announcement of the winner would come over the intercom during the last period.

Gayle won. I was in science when the announcements were made. I guess I shouldn't have been surprised. But something must have shown on my face, because Flip was looking at me oddly.

"I'm glad Gayle won," I lied, "but don't you think Peggy made a better speech?"

Flip nodded. "If it wasn't for The Club, I'd have voted for her myself. But you know, it's really just a popularity contest."

I tried not to feel too bad. After all, I *had* helped Peggy. And I'd only betrayed her a tiny bit. It probably wouldn't have mattered anyway. Gayle still would have won.

But she'd be a crummy treasurer. And maybe if I'd worked a little harder for Peggy, maybe if I hadn't spent so much time at Gayle's, maybe if I'd had the guts to confront them all and tell them why Peggy would be better, she might have won.

All those maybe-ifs. None of them mattered. There was nothing I could do about it now.

Chapter 7

For the sin which we have committed before Thee by idle gossip . . .

"Have you got good notes?" Flip asked as we left school on a sunny June afternoon. "Mine stink."

"They're okay," I replied. "I've tried to write down everything Mr. Hodges says in class. I just wish I understood what I was writing. Science is not my best subject."

"Mine either. Come to think of it, I don't even have a best subject."

"You're good in phys ed," I reminded her.

"Yeah, that'll be my one and only A. Too bad it won't impress my parents. My father's always reminding me that there aren't many career opportunities in volleyball." Flip deepened her voice as she said this and affected a stern expression that made me laugh.

I liked Flip. She was my favorite of all The Club girls, the only one I saw away from school and the mall. She was down-to-earth and easygoing, and she never made a point of reminding me that I wasn't an official member of the crowd yet. And she made me laugh. She frequently ignored The Club's rule about gossip, and sometimes told me really funny stories about the other girls. Nothing major, just silly little things, like the fact that Janet, who always seemed so mature, looked in her closet and under her bed every night before going to sleep.

But Flip was spacey, definitely spacey. Here we were, just going into final exam week, and she had just realized she hadn't exactly been keeping up. The science exam was tomorrow. So I was going home with her to study together. For the next few hours, I was supposed to cram a whole semester's worth of science into her head. I didn't mind. Much as I hated the class, being lab partners with Flip had made it tolerable, even fun sometimes.

"Hi, Mom," Flip called out as we walked into the kitchen. Her mother was emptying the dishwasher.

"Hi, Mrs. Duval," I said.

She smiled, but put a finger to her lips. "I just got the baby to sleep."

"We're going to my room to study," Flip whispered. She opened the refrigerator and pulled out a six-pack of sodas. "You want potato chips or pretzels? Or both?"

"I'm on a diet," I told her.

"Why? You're not fat."

I *really* liked Flip.

Armed with sodas and two bags we went up to her room. "Ooh, that's nice," I said, admiring the dress lying on her bed. The tags were still attached to the dark green T-shirt dress splashed with abstract purple spots.

"Thanks," Flip said. "I got it for Saturday." She picked it up and held it against her. "But Dani says it's too outrageous for a rush party."

My heart quickened. "Rush party?"

"Yeah, for The Club. To pick new members. We decided to have it right after school's out before people go away for the summer." She laid the dress back down on the bed. "Are you coming?"

I swallowed. "Am I invited?"

"Sure."

I was floating.

"Anyone can come," she added.

I came back down to earth.

"We're going to start spreading the word to-morrow," she continued. "As soon as we decide where it's going to be. Probably at Dani's."

I sat down on the edge of her bed and looked at her dress. "What should I wear?"

"Anything you want," Flip said, ripping open the bag of potato chips. She extended it toward me.

I took one and chewed it without even tasting it. "I've got a new Laura Ashley dress. Pink flowers."

Flip flopped down on the other bed and crammed a handful of chips in her mouth. "Sounds nice."

"Dani will probably think it's babyish."

"So what? If you like it, wear it. What do you care what Dani thinks?"

I looked pointedly at the T-shirt dress. "Oh yeah? Maybe you should take your own advice."

"What do you mean?"

"You just said, Dani thinks this is too outrageous for the party."

Flip grinned. "But I'm going to wear it anyway."

"You are? Even if Dani doesn't like it?"

Flip fell back on her bed, oblivious to the potato chip crumbs dropping onto her bedspread. "Yeah. I'm sick of the way Dani tries to run my life. And everyone else's." Then she sat up. "But if I don't pass this exam, my parents are going to start running my life. And I'll be spending the rest of it in this room."

I forced the rush party out of my head and opened my notebook. "Yeah, we better get going." I flipped through some pages. "I guess we should start with the parts of the body. Bones first."

Flip opened a soda and handed it to me. "Arms and legs, fingers and toes," she chanted as she opened one for herself.

"Get serious," I ordered. "What's a fibula?"

Flip considered this. "A little tiny white lie?"

"Flip!" I read from the notes. "It's the bone on the outer side of the lower part of the leg."

Flip nodded. "The bone on the lower side of the outer part of the leg."

This was going to be harder than I'd thought. I tried an easier one. "What's a tibia?"

"The bone next to the fibula?"

"Well, sort of. It's the shinbone. What's an ulna?"

"What's the point?" Flip moaned. "Bones. As long as they're not broken, who cares what they're called?"

"Mr. Hodges cares," I replied. "So you better start caring, too. Now, what's an ulna?"

It seemed to ring a bell. "Something in the arm?"

"Good! It's the thinner bone. By the way, did you get the notes from last Friday when I was absent?"

Flip grabbed her notebook. "Yeah, they're here somewhere. I copied them from the guy who sits behind us." She squinted at a piece of paper. "Only now I can't read what I wrote."

"Let me see."

As I studied the paper, Flip asked, "What was the matter with you Friday? Were you sick?"

"Just cramps. I get fierce ones sometimes."

"Yuck. That must be awful."

"Don't you get cramps?" When she didn't reply immediately, I looked up from my notes.

Flip appeared to be fascinated by the list of ingredients on the pretzel bag. Then she gave me a funny sort of abashed smile. "I don't even have my period yet."

"You're kidding!" I blurted out before I could

stop myself. Then I didn't know what to say. "I'm sorry."

"It's not your fault," Flip said. "And it's not like there's anything wrong with me. I'll get it sooner or later. My mother said she didn't get hers till she was sixteen."

Her tone was nonchalant but she still looked a little embarrassed. "Listen, you're lucky," I said quickly. "It's a real drag every month."

But I was actually floored. I didn't know anyone in the eighth grade who didn't have her period. Of course, maybe I did and just didn't know about it. It wasn't as if we talked about periods all that much.

I went back to the notes, but my eyes kept darting up to Flip. It was amazing to me. Here she looked so cool and trendy and sophisticated, but she wasn't even a woman yet. Appearances certainly could be deceiving.

Normally, the first day of summer vacation, I'd be on a major high. Exams were over, and I'd done okay. I had almost three months of no classes and no homework to look forward to. I should have been feeling positively euphoric.

Not that Saturday, though. There should be a new word for the kind of nervousness I was feeling.

My hands trembled as I fumbled with the buttons on the back of my jumpsuit. Finally I went to the door and yelled, "Mom, help me!"

I'd almost worn my Laura Ashley, but I chickened out at the last moment. Maybe once I was actually in The Club, like Flip, I wouldn't be so intimidated by Dani.

My mother came in. "What's the problem?"

"Can you button this for me?"

"What kind of party is this anyway?" she asked as she went to work.

"It's a tea party."

"A tea party? Is that some new fad?"

"No." I went to my drawer for the matching belt. "It's for a club."

"What kind of club?"

"Just a club." But even as I spoke, I knew there was no point in even trying to be evasive. Once my mother was interested in finding out something, nothing could stop her.

"What's it called?" she asked.

I wasn't about to give in quickly. "The Club."

She exhaled one of her aggravated sighs. "And what does The Club do?"

I was setting out makeup on my dresser, and I eyed her reflection through the mirror. "Mom, did you ever consider becoming a lawyer? You'd be great at cross-examination."

"Very funny." She sat down on my bed. "I'm not

prying, Mindy, I'm just interested. I know you're not getting involved in anything . . . bad."

For a moment, I debated teasing her, letting her think The Club was some sort of wild street gang. But I really wasn't in the mood for games.

"It's just a group of girls. They're having this party to choose new members."

I was mildly alarmed when her brow furrowed. "But what's the basis for their selection? Is it a hobby or something like that?"

"It's just a group of girls who hang out together, that's all."

The lines on her forehead deepened. "You mean, it's like a sorority?"

"Sort of," I admitted.

I heard another sigh. "Oh, Mindy."

I turned away from the mirror and faced her. "What?"

She shook her head. "I don't like those kinds of clubs, where people are excluded."

I put my hands on my hips. "You act like you think I'm going to be one of the people excluded."

She took on an expression that infuriated me. "I just don't want to see you get hurt." It was as if she was already feeling sorry for me.

I stamped my foot. Pretty childish, but I couldn't help it. "It's no wonder I don't have any self-confidence! You just automatically assume I won't get picked!"

My outburst startled her. "Honey, it's not that." She seemed to be struggling for the right words. "It's just that, well, I hope getting into this club isn't too important to you. Clubs like this, they don't have any real reasons for who they pick and who they leave out. And people get hurt—"

"Well, maybe, just maybe, I won't be one of the hurt ones," I interrupted. "Did that ever occur to you?"

She uttered an "I give up" sigh. And she got up. "I hope you're right." But she didn't look very convinced as she left the room.

For a moment I just stood there, and waited for the anger and the anxiety and the tension to drain from my body. I took one last look into the mirror. And then, with grim determination, I left the room and walked out of the house without even saying good-bye.

I could have asked my mother to drive me to Dani's. But I didn't want to be alone in the car with her, a captive audience. So I walked. It wasn't that far. I just hoped I wouldn't sweat too much.

I'd never seen Dani's house before. I guess I'd expected something really fabulous, like a mansion. It was just an ordinary split-level brick house, not much different from mine. As I walked up the driveway, a car pulled up alongside. Kelly jumped out.

"Hi," she said.

"Hi," I replied. And we walked toward the house in silence. I was dying to ask her if she was nervous, but then she'd know I was.

Dani opened the door. She was actually smiling, but it was the phoniest smile I'd ever seen. It was probably her idea of how the perfect gracious hostess should smile. She ushered us through the foyer into the living room.

I counted about fifteen girls, gathered in small groups, speaking in hushed tones. I knew all but two. At least six of them weren't already in The Club. I wished I knew how many they were planning to take in.

"There are refreshments in the dining room," Dani informed us. Kelly went with her in that direction, but I stayed put. I had this fear of spilling tea or talking with my mouth full. Or getting something caught between my teeth.

I looked around for Flip, but I didn't see her, so I joined a group that included Lisa and Gayle. It was so weird. Here were these girls I saw all the time, five, sometimes six times a week. And I felt like I was meeting total strangers.

They were acting like that, too. "Oh, hello, Mindy," Gayle said. "What a cute outfit."

"Thank you," I replied. "You look very nice, too.

And so do you, Lisa," I added hastily, although Lisa looked like she always did, dressed entirely in black.

"Thank you," Lisa said.

"You're welcome." Above the hum of conversation, I could hear Kelly's voice. "Dani, these cookies are absolutely delicious."

"Mindy, this is Andrea Hollis," Gayle said.

"Pleased to meet you," I said to the pretty girl with long brown curly hair. "I haven't seen you around school."

"I just moved to Fox Haven," Andrea said.

"She's living right next door to me," Gayle added.

My smile grew thinner.

"Where's Flip?" I asked.

"She's not coming," Lisa told me. "Her parents had to go somewhere and the baby-sitter cancelled at the last minute. So she had to stay home with her baby brother."

"Oh, that's too bad." I turned to Andrea. "Flip and I were lab partners this year. It was great fun."

"Fun?" Lisa made a face. "In science?"

"Well, you know how Flip is. We got really silly. You should have seen us when we were dissecting the frog. I'd just cut its stomach open when Flip—"

"Mindy!" Gayle indicated the plate of cookies she was holding. "Not while I'm eating!"

"Oh. Sorry."

Andrea peered at me over the rim of her tea cup as she took a delicate sip. Now I wished I *had* taken something to eat or drink, anything to hold onto. My hands were getting sweaty.

Out of the corner of my eye, I saw Dani ushering two non-Club girls into the room. More competition. Janet came by and whispered in Gayle's ear before moving on.

"Dani wants us to mingle," Gayle told Lisa.

"I think I'll get more tea," Andrea murmured.

I considered following her, but decided I'd be better off spending the time with people who counted. I moved through the room, stopping every few seconds to tell a Club member how much I liked her dress, or her earrings, or her shoes, or her hair—whatever I could think of. I would have felt like a major phony, except for the fact that they were all doing the same thing. I've never had so many compliments in my life.

I missed Flip. She would have treated this whole business like a big joke.

I found myself face to face with Dani. "You have a lovely home."

"My mother just redecorated," she said.

"She has fabulous taste," I gushed.

Dani smiled, nodded, and moved on. Now where to go? I passed through the dining room, and paused to admire the display of cookies and tiny sandwiches. I didn't trust the condition of my stomach enough to eat anything, though.

Beyond the dining room, I could see into the kitchen. Lisa was there, with Janet and Kelly at the breakfast table. I tried to catch someone's eye, but they had their heads together. Finally I just walked in and took the fourth seat at the table.

"I *know*," Kelly was saying as I sat down. "I *saw* her."

"Saw who?" I asked.

Lisa checked over her shoulder. Then she leaned in closer to me. "Do you know that girl with the short black hair and long dangly earrings?"

Kelly supplied the name. "Karen Bell."

I nodded. "Yeah, what about her?"

Lisa's lips twitched. "Did you notice her legs?"

"She doesn't shave them," Kelly whispered. "It's gross."

I made the appropriate expression of horror. At least that was one girl I wouldn't have to worry about.

"Speaking of hair," Janet said, "do you know Beth Leonard?"

"She's in my phys ed class," I said. "Doesn't she shave her legs either?"

"This is better," Janet announced. "You're not going to believe what I found out about her." She paused dramatically.

"Tell us," Lisa demanded.

"She has a mustache."

"You're kidding!" I exclaimed. "I never noticed that."

Janet smiled smugly. "That's because she takes it off."

"You mean, she *shaves?*" Kelly squealed.

"Shh," Janet hissed. "No, I think she uses a cream or something."

"Yuck," Lisa commented.

"Really," I agreed. I was starting to relax. This felt good, sitting here all cozy and conspiratorial. I wished I had a little piece of gossip to offer. The only item I could think of was Janet's habit of looking in the closet and under the bed before going to sleep. Obviously, I couldn't share that.

"Maybe Beth should lend some of that cream to Señora Schultz," Kelly remarked.

We all giggled at that. The Spanish teacher was pretty hairy. "I always think she's really a man disguised as a woman," I said.

"No way," Lisa said. "I was by her desk once and the bottom drawer was open. She must have unbelievable periods. There were a zillion tampons in there. *Super* size."

"Speaking of periods," Kelly said, "do you know about Cathy Becker?" I could tell from the glint in her eyes that this was going to be good.

"She lives down the street from me," Kelly continued. "Last week I went over there to copy her English notes. Anyway, while I was sitting there writing, I felt like I was getting my period. So I asked her if I could borrow a tampon or a pad. And you know what she said?"

We waited with bated breath.

"She said she'd get one from her mother's bathroom."

Lisa stared at her blankly. "So?"

"Don't you get it? *She* doesn't have her period yet!" Kelly leaned back in her chair with an attitude of triumph. I couldn't blame her. Lisa and Janet were very impressed, and I was seething with envy.

"She's already fourteen!" Janet exclaimed.

"Wow," Lisa murmured. "I don't know anyone our age who doesn't have her period yet."

"I do," I said suddenly. For once, all eyes were on me, and they all gleamed in expectation.

"Who?" they asked in unison.

"Flip."

Disbelief was clearly evident on all three faces.

"It's true," I insisted. "She told me."

I waited. But this time there were no shrieks, no squeals, no giggles. Janet and Lisa glanced at each other, and then just as quickly looked away. Kelly suddenly became very interested in her fingernails.

Then Janet pushed her chair away from the table. "We better get back to the living room. Dani wants us to mingle."

Kelly got up and followed her out. Lisa paused by my chair, but she didn't look at me when she spoke. "Look, Mindy, don't spread that around about Flip, okay?" She didn't wait for my reply.

I sat there for a second, alone. Dimly, I was aware of a coldness that seemed to penetrate my entire body.

Somehow, I managed to get up. And like a robot, I went back to join the party.

"Valerie, get off the phone!"

She shook her head and spoke into the receiver. "Then what happened?"

"I'm expecting a call!"

The little monster stuck out her tongue, and her grip on the phone tightened.

"Mom!" I shrieked.

My father ambled into the kitchen and opened the freezer. "She's not home," he said.

"Dad, Valerie's been on the phone for an hour!"

Valerie moved her mouth from the receiver just long enough to say, "Have not."

"Don't tie up the phone, Val," my father said, pulling out a carton of ice cream.

"Dad, make her get off!"

But he was gazing into the carton with a sad expression. "Who put an empty carton of ice cream in the freezer?"

"It was her," I accused, pointing to the thing attached to the telephone. "Why don't you send her to her room till she's five feet tall?"

My father's voice was mournful. "And I had a craving for ice cream. Who wants to go to the Soda Shoppe?"

That got some reaction. Within seconds, I was

alone in the house. I sat down at the kitchen table and stared at the phone, willing it to ring.

They were choosing the new members today. I wasn't supposed to know this, but I did. Flip called me yesterday, right after I got home from the rush party. She said the new members would get a call right after the meeting.

I had something else to worry about, too. Would Janet or Lisa tell her that I'd exposed her secret? Of course, she hadn't actually said it was a secret. She hadn't made me promise not to tell or anything like that. And Flip was just as big a gossip as anyone.

I looked at the clock. It was five after three. They were meeting right that minute. Even as I sat there, my name was being tossed around, debated. I felt like someone on trial, waiting for the jury to come out.

I got up and began wandering around the house. I had to do something to pass the time. I could watch TV—but what if I didn't hear the telephone? Or I could read, but I knew I wouldn't be able to concentrate.

Finally I went up to my room and began reorganizing my dresser drawers. I pulled out everything—sweaters, T-shirts, slips, underwear. Then, slowly and carefully, I folded each item. I arranged piles on the bed. Then I put everything back in the drawers.

Then I rearranged my jewelry box, separating necklaces and bracelets and earrings, and putting them in different compartments.

After that, I did the closet. When I finished, all the blouses were together, and so were the skirts, the dresses, and the pants. Shoes were placed on the floor in a perfectly aligned row.

It seemed as if only moments had passed. But when I went back to the kitchen and looked at the clock, I was stunned. It was almost five. And the phone hadn't rung.

I ran back upstairs to my parents' room, to make sure that extension wasn't off the cradle. It looked fine. I picked it up and heard a dial tone. Quickly, I replaced it.

I heard a door downstairs open, and a moment later my mother's voice. "Anyone home?"

I left her room and met her on the stairs. "Just me. Dad took Valerie for ice cream."

"Why didn't you go?" she asked.

"I'm waiting for a phone call."

"Oh." She must have heard something in my tone, because she looked at me curiously for a moment. When I didn't offer any more information, she went on up to her bedroom.

I returned to the kitchen. Silently, I screamed at the phone, "Ring!" But nothing happened.

I couldn't stand it any longer. I picked up the receiver and dialed Flip's number. "Hi, Mrs. Duval, this is Mindy. Is Flip home?"

"No, she's at a Club meeting, Mindy. I'll tell her you called."

"Thank you." I hung up and grabbed the phone directory. Then I dialed another number.

A child's voice answered. "Hello?" I remembered Kelly saying she had a six-year-old sister.

"Is Kelly there?"

"No."

"Um, do you know where she is?"

"No. Someone called her and she was all excited and she ran out. She's in a club."

"When . . . when did she leave?"

"I don't know. Mommy! When did Kelly leave?" In the background I heard a faint response. Then the little girl said, "Couple of hours ago."

"Thank you." I hung up the phone.

It was weird. I wasn't feeling anything at all. It was like my whole body was numb.

"Mindy?" My mother was standing in the doorway. "Are you still waiting for your phone call?"

I didn't want her to know she had been right. I didn't want her pity, her sympathy, or her understanding. "No. There won't be any call."

I knew she wanted to say something. She knew there was nothing I wanted to hear. But I couldn't make her leave. And I couldn't move. I couldn't stop the tears from streaming down my face, either. And I didn't even try to push her away when she wrapped her arms around me.

Chapter 8

For the sin which we have committed before Thee
by unchastity . . .

Mindy, did you pack your bathing suit?"

I simply could not dignify my mother's question
with a response. Did she honestly think I'd pack for
two weeks at the beach and forget my bathing suit?
But just to be on the safe side, I ran my hands through
the stuff piled in the suitcase.

She must have had some weird sixth sense or
something. Quickly, I pulled my suit out of a drawer
and stuffed it in the case.

"Okay, everyone, let's load up the car!" my father
yelled. I grabbed my bag and my Walkman and headed
downstairs. Outside, my parents were shoving the
suitcases and folded beach chairs into the car trunk.
Valerie was already in the backseat, her lap covered
with stuff—travel games, a pack of cards, a bag of
grapes.

I handed my father my suitcase and got in the
other side of the back. Immediately, I clamped my

headset over my ears, in order to make it perfectly clear that I would not be participating in any stupid car games or sing-alongs during the two-and-a-half-hour drive.

Even with my ears covered, I could hear the traditional family cry as Dad backed out of the driveway. "One, two, three, we're off!" I didn't join in, but I couldn't help feeling the familiar tingle of anticipation, a feeling I'd had every summer that I could remember.

We were on our way to Ocean Point. Every summer, my family rented a cottage there for two weeks. My mother's two sisters and their families took cottages, too. It was just a little beach town, not a fancy resort or anything, but I'd always had fun there. Besides, Ocean Point could have been the biggest dump in the universe, and it would still be better than staying here.

Three weeks had passed since I didn't get into The Club. Three weeks of television, reading, and generally sitting around the house feeling miserable. My mother was sympathetic for a while, but then she started nagging me to get out and do something.

But do what? And go where? I didn't dare go to the mall or the swimming pool. I might run into one of The Club girls there. I couldn't even hang out at Peggy's—she was off at gymnastics camp.

I hadn't heard from any of my former so-called friends, not even Flip. I thought about calling her, to find out why exactly I hadn't gotten in. But the fact that she hadn't called me led me to suspect she might know that I told the others about her not having her period. That might even have been the reason why I didn't get in. Or maybe they just never really liked me.

The tape on my Walkman ended, and my ears were starting to feel sore, so I took the headset off.

"Wanna play a game?" Valerie asked hopefully.

"Not particularly," I replied.

"Oh, Mindy, play with her," my mother urged.

Valerie began setting up the magnetic checkers set. "I'm getting good at this," she said. "I bet I'll beat you."

"I'm trembling with fear," I said. At least checkers didn't require much concentration. I could think about the beach and my plans for the next two weeks.

My mother's two sisters were Aunt Margie and Aunt Susan. Aunt Margie was married to Uncle Bob, and they had two kids, Joannie, who would be fifteen now, and Gary, who about nine. Aunt Susan and Uncle Harry had David, sixteen, Jeff, who was twelve, and Sarah, who was ten, like Valerie.

Valerie played with Sarah and Gary, and I used to hang around with Jeff. Not this year, though. This summer I planned to be with David and Joannie.

Okay, they were older, but not that much. They'd

never paid attention to me before, but things were different now. I wasn't a child anymore. I was almost fourteen. With makeup, I could pass for fifteen, maybe even sixteen. At twelve, Jeff was probably still a little kid. Besides, everyone knew that girls matured faster than boys.

No, this summer I'd hang out with my older cousins and their friends. I'd be with them at the twice-a-week movies on the beach at night, and the once-a-week dances at the community center.

"King me, king me," Valerie chanted. I complied. I hadn't even noticed that she'd jumped half my men. I was too busy picturing myself with Joannie, David, and their friends, hanging out on the beach, playing volleyball, looking like someone in a television commercial for diet soda.

Three games later, I started smelling the salt in the air. "We're here, we're here," Valerie shrieked, bouncing up and down in her seat. I gazed out the window at the familiar sights floating by—trim white cottages with screened-in porches, a fried-clam bar, the community center. Between the cottages I caught glimpses of the sandy beach and the white-tipped waves kicking at the shore.

We pulled up in front of one of the little cottages. For the next hour and a half, we raced around performing the annual routine—unloading the car, opening windows to get the musty smell out of the house, unpacking, making up the beds. And then we were ready to walk down the road to Aunt Susan's for the family reunion.

The cottage that Aunt Susan and Uncle Harry took was the biggest, and it was the gathering place. Once inside, there was the usual flurry of hugs and kisses, everyone talking at once.

"Hey, Mindy Mouse," Jeff said. I winced, hearing the nickname he'd given me when we were really little. I used to call him Jeffy Pop, like the popcorn.

He looked exactly the same, short and scrawny and a little goofy. He tried to give me the secret handshake we'd invented three summers ago, but I couldn't remember exactly how to do it. "We brought Nintendo," he informed me.

It was less than thrilling news, but I smiled kindly. "That's nice. Where's Joannie?"

He made a face. "Out back. Why?"

"Just want to say hello." I went through the house and out the back door. They didn't see me right away, which gave me a chance to look them over.

Joannie was in the center of a group consisting of two other girls and two boys. I almost didn't recognize her. The last time I saw her she had short brown hair. Now it was long and streaked blond. What really blew me away was her figure and the way she was showing it off in super-tight shorts and a teensy halter. The other girls were similarly dressed. Furtively, I tucked my T-shirt into my baggy cutoffs. Then I checked out the boys.

It was a shock to realize one of them was David. I couldn't tell if he'd actually grown, or what, but he seemed so much older. His sleeveless shirt revealed actual muscles. And he looked like he shaved.

The other guy was incredibly good looking, like a surfer. He had blond hair and a serious tan.

"Hi," I said. And then, louder, I tried again. "Hi."

There were no hugs and kisses this time, but David grinned at me. "Hiya, kid, how's it going?"

Joannie's mouth formed a brief imitation of a smile. "Hi, Mindy." Then she turned to the other girls. "Want something to drink?" She didn't even bother to introduce me as they swept past and into the cottage.

At least David had some manners. "This is my cousin Mindy," he told his friend. "Mindy, this is Larry."

Larry flashed a brief smile and said, "Nice meeting you, Mandy."

"Mindy," I corrected him, but I wasn't sure he heard me.

A few moments later, everyone was out back. The grill was smoking, and the picnic table was laden with salads and sodas. Joannie and David and their friends had settled on a blanket, away from the parents and the little ones.

I collected a hamburger, potato salad, and a soda.

Then I headed over to the blanket and planted myself next to Joannie.

"I love your hair," I said. "I've been thinking about doing something like that."

Joannie's girlfriend eyed me with unconcealed amusement. "Don't you think you're a little young to color your hair?"

I laughed as if she'd just made a huge joke. Joannie glanced at me. "Your mother would kill you." Then she turned back to her friend and they started talking as if I wasn't even there.

I made another attempt, this time with David. "How's school?"

"Fine," he said. "How about you? Still making all A's?"

I rolled my eyes. "Hardly. There's so much else going on."

"Better keep up your marks," he said, sounding like my father. "Where's Jeff?"

"How should I know?"

He shrugged. "I thought you two were inseparable." Then he turned to the others. "Eat up, guys. If we're going to make that movie in town, we'll have to get going."

"What movie?" I asked.

"Hey, Mindy!" I turned to see Jeff waving at me.

"I think you're being summoned," David said.

"I got the Nintendo set up!" Jeff yelled.

All around me, the older ones were getting up

and brushing crumbs away. "Have fun," David's handsome friend said. And they all took off.

Well, I was getting a fantastic tan. Mainly because there was nothing else for me to do but lie on the beach and bake. If I ended up with skin cancer, it was all their fault.

Down the beach, I could see David and Joannie and their buddies playing volleyball. Up on the road, the ice cream truck had just pulled up. In the crowd gathered around it, I saw Valerie with Sarah and Gary.

And here I was. Caught in the middle.

"Want to get an ice cream?"

I blinked at Jeff. "No thanks."

"Want to look for crabs down by the jetty?"

"No."

"Okay." He ambled off. At least he wasn't taking my neglect to heart. That was a nice thing about Jeff. He wasn't the type who got hurt easily. And he had other friends around. Besides, he could probably see that I'd outgrown him.

I lay back on the towel. The sun penetrated my eyelids, so even with my eyes closed I saw brightness. Then a shadow passed over. Someone was standing over me.

"Jeff, you're blocking the sun."

"Who's Jeff?"

I opened my eyes. A boy was standing there. "Hi," he said.

I stared at him dumbly. He indicated the spot next to me. "This sand taken?"

I shook my head. He sat down. "What's your name?"

"Mindy."

"I'm Patrick. How long have you been here?"

"A week."

"You've been lying on this spot for a week?"

It wasn't very funny, but I smiled anyway. He was kind of cute. Not gorgeous, but not bad either. Brown hair, brown eyes, average build. And he looked at least fifteen. "I've been here three days," he said. "The three most boring days of my life."

I sat up. "Is this your first summer in Ocean Point?"

"Yeah. Hope it's the last." Then he gave me a crooked grin. "Only now I'm thinking maybe it's not going to be so bad after all. Who's this Jeff person?"

"Just a cousin."

His grin broadened. "That's good."

It dawned on me that he was flirting.

"Where are you from?" I asked.

"Pennsylvania. Near Philadelphia."

"I'm from Fox Haven."

"Where's that?"

"Here. Connecticut, I mean." I was dying to know how old he was. "What class are you in?"

"Senior."

A senior. That meant he was seventeen. I could barely breathe. A seventeen-year-old boy was flirting with me.

"What about you?"

"I'm . . . a junior."

He bought it. He didn't bat an eye. "You come here a lot?"

"My parents take a cottage for two weeks every summer."

"Anything to do around here besides get a tan?"

"Not much," I replied. "There's a community center. They've got arts and crafts—"

He snorted.

"For the little kids," I added hastily. "They have dances sometimes."

That got a slightly more interested reaction. I gazed out at the water. "There's one tonight."

"Yeah? You going?"

I examined a mosquito bite on my knee. "Maybe." I could feel his eyes.

"Got a date?"

"Not really." And then I remembered a look I'd once seen Dani use on a boy. Keeping my face forward, I lowered my head, and eyed him sideways. He grinned.

"Mindy!" Valerie's shriek killed the atmosphere. "Mom says come on, we're going back!"

"Kid sister?" Patrick asked.

"Pet frog," I replied.

He laughed. Then he got up. "Well, maybe I'll see you at the dance tonight."

I nodded. I waited till he'd walked away before I got up, mainly because I was afraid to move. I thought he'd see my whole body shake. This was almost a date! And it was too perfect for words. I'd be seen by my older cousins at the dance with a seventeen-year-old.

And I wouldn't even have to tell my parents. Not that they'd forbid me to go or anything like that. But if they knew I was meeting a boy there, they'd want to know about him. And I didn't think they'd be too crazy about the idea of my being with a boy four years older.

But one of the nicest things about being in Ocean Point was that my parents were a lot looser here than they were back in Fox Haven. They didn't cross-examine me on where I was going, who I was meeting, when I'd be getting back. So when they left that evening to go play cards at Aunt Susan's, taking Valerie with them, I just casually announced I was meeting friends at the community center. There were no objections.

Still, I was glad they were out of the cottage. If my mother witnessed the preparations I was about to make, she'd definitely get suspicious.

I showered, washed my hair, dried it, and spent about forty-five minutes on my makeup. And it wasn't my usual makeup. Black eyeliner, maroon lipstick—my mother would have had a fit. I put on my cropped pants with a long flowered shirt. Then I took a long, hard look at myself in the mirror.

I could pass for sixteen. Or at least fifteen—and that was the age you were supposed to be to go to the community center dances.

I could hear the music as I approached the community center. My stomach jumped when I recognized the guy taking admission at the door. He was one of the regular lifeguards on the beach. Only a few years ago he'd seen me with a Donald Duck inner tube around my waist.

But there wasn't the slightest hint of recognition in his eyes when he took my dollar. And that bolstered my confidence as I walked in.

It took a moment before my eyes adjusted to the dim lighting. I didn't see Patrick among the kids dancing and hanging around the soda counter. But I did see my cousin Joannie with her friends. And she saw me.

She actually left her friends and came over. "What are you doing here?" She was looking at me as if I was a three-year-old who had wandered into a bar.

"It's a free country," I replied with nonchalance. Bad comeback.

Joannie's eyes were reproving. "You're not supposed to be here. You have to be fifteen."

This motherly bit, coming from someone who was only slightly over a year older than me, was getting extremely annoying. "What are you going to do about it?" I asked. "Have me arrested?"

Her lips tightened. "Well, I hope you're not planning to tag along with me," she said.

I dismissed that notion with a blithe wave of my hand. "I'm meeting someone. A guy."

I could tell she didn't believe me. But it was my lucky day. There he was, coming right toward me. The timing couldn't have been better.

"Patrick, hi!" And I had the wonderful satisfaction of seeing Joannie's mouth drop open as I brushed right past her. I wasn't going to introduce her for three very good reasons. One, she never bothered to introduce me to her friends. Two, she was too good looking. And most important, three—I didn't want to run the risk of her telling him my real age.

"You look good," Patrick said.

"Thanks." He didn't look half-bad himself. In the dim light, he was cuter than on the beach. He wore jeans, ripped in exactly the right places, and a T-shirt from the last Rolling Stones tour with the sleeves torn off.

"Want to dance?" he asked.

I hadn't danced publicly much, but I'd watched a lot of Madonna videos and I'd practiced a lot in front of the mirror at home. We danced straight through four songs. I was limp.

"I need something to drink," I said.

Patrick cocked his head toward the refreshment stand. "What have they got over there?"

"Sodas and juice."

"I can do better than that," Patrick said. He pulled a flask out of his back pocket.

"Fantastic!" I exclaimed, hoping Joannie could see us.

But just as Patrick was unscrewing the cap, a man appeared. "Hey! No alcohol in here!"

I recognized him. He'd been the arts and crafts director ever since the days when I was in this room making potholders.

"Aw, give me a break," Pat muttered, but he screwed the cap back on.

The man was staring at me. "Aren't you the little Wise girl?" He was distracted by some yelling from the other side of the room.

With some urgency, I said, "Let's get out of here."

Outside the center, Patrick leaned against the lamppost. He took out the flask. "Ladies first."

I took a tiny sip. It tasted horrible, and it burned going down my throat. I started to hand it back when I saw Joannie and her girlfriend coming outside. I stepped into the light and held the flask to my lips. "Mmm."

Joannie and her friend were watching. I extended the flask toward him. As he reached out to take it,

I lightly stroked his arm with my other hand. It would probably have been more effective if I had long fingernails.

But it did have an effect nonetheless. He took a gulp from the flask. His other hand was moving through my hair.

I smiled. His hand moved down the back of my neck. Then he pulled my face toward him and he kissed me. I could feel his tongue pressing against my clenched lips.

I pulled back. "Not *here*."

I looked back at the center entrance. Joannie and her friend were gone. But then I saw someone else coming toward the building. It was my cousin David and his friend Larry.

Patrick had his hand on my neck again. "Don't," I whispered. "My cousin's coming. Hide the flask!"

He shoved it back in his pocket.

"Mindy?"

"Hi, David. Uh, Patrick, this is my cousin David, and this is Larry."

The guys shook hands. As the light from the lamp hit David's face, I detected a quizzical expression. I figured he was too polite to ask me what I was doing with this older boy, but I had a feeling he was wondering.

"Going to the dance?" Larry asked.

"We've been," I said. I saw the top of the flask

sticking out of Patrick's pocket. I moved in closer to him to block David's view. "We just came out for some air."

David's eyes darted back and forth between me and Patrick. I had a sinking suspicion he could smell liquor on Patrick's breath. Or worse, on mine.

"Larry!" A girl was standing by the center door, beckoning.

"Let's go on in," Larry said to David.

"Right," he replied. "See you guys." But he kept turning and glancing back as he walked to the door.

"What's his problem?" Patrick asked.

"Oh, just because he's . . . a little older, he treats me like I'm a kid."

"So what do you want to do now?" he asked.

I considered the possibilities. There weren't many. "Are you hungry? The clam bar's still open. And the ice cream place."

"Isn't there a bar by the grocery store?"

"Yeah, but you have to be twenty-one."

"Don't you have a fake ID?" His tone put it in the same category as a social security card.

"Oh sure," I lied, "but I don't have it with me." Then I got an inspiration. "Why don't we walk along Stony Beach?"

"What's Stony Beach?"

"You know, the beach with all the rocks, where nobody swims. At least I won't run into any cousins there. It's pretty deserted at night."

Patrick grinned. "Yeah, okay." We started down the road.

"You're going to be a senior this fall, right?"

"Yeah."

"Are you applying to colleges?"

"Sure. But I've got to get decent SAT scores. My grades stink."

"SAT?" I repeated.

"The exams. For getting into college. Don't you know what SAT's are?"

"Oh sure, sure." I did my sideways look. "I guess I had my mind on . . . other things." I gave him a sidelong smile.

I must have been getting good at this. He put an arm around my shoulder. We walked down the steps that led from the road to the beach.

By the time we got to the bottom, his arm was getting heavy, but I resisted the impulse to shrug it off. Even in my discomfort, I was aware of how lovely the beach looked. It was absolutely deserted, no screaming kids or blaring tape decks. The lights from the road above offered just enough illumination, making the waves sparkle and casting a glow on the sand and rocks.

The only sound was the rush of the ocean, the slapping of waves on the shore. It was all terribly romantic. And here I was, with a real boy. I almost wished someone would jump out from behind a rock with a camera, so I could capture this moment forever.

"I walk out here around twilight sometimes," I told Patrick. "See that huge rock? It's got a carved-out space in it like a chair. I like to sit there and look out at the ocean."

"Yeah? Think two would fit?"

"Maybe. We could try."

Patrick climbed into it first, and I squeezed in next to him. It was a tight fit.

I'd never been so physically close to a boy before. I could hear my heart thumping. I wondered if he could.

He didn't even have to pull me closer to press his lips against mine. Then he drew back. "Is that how you always kiss?"

I wasn't sure what he meant. I giggled. "Uh, tell me where you're applying to college."

"Don't know yet." His face was moving in again.

"What are you going to major in?"

"Don't know. Hey, you talk too much."

"I was just curious—" That's all I got out before his mouth was clamped down on mine. And this time I could feel his tongue. It was slimy.

His hands were moving. One was stroking my neck, the other going up and down my back. Mine were just hanging limp. Awkwardly, I maneuvered them around his chest.

A hand crept under my shirt. I felt the cold metal of his watch moving up my bare skin. Then he detached his mouth, and started kissing my neck. Or licking it. I shuddered.

He misinterpreted that. "You like this . . ." he murmured.

"What . . . what time is it?"

"What do you care?"

"I just . . . I mean . . . I want to know."

He actually took his hand away to look. "Almost ten." Then it went right back to where it had been.

Almost ten. At Aunt Susan's, Jeff was turning on the television. Last summer I was there every night at ten. That was when the old "Brady Bunch" reruns were on. In a couple of minutes Jeff would be watching Cindy and Marcia and Greg and Jan and Bobby and—what was the middle Brady boy named? It began with a P.

I gasped. He'd undone my bra hook. And a hand was moving around toward my chest. Any minute now . . .

"Stop that!"

The terror in my voice came through loud and clear. "What?"

"Don't do that!" Frantic, I scrambled off the rock. I stuck my hands behind my back and fumbled with the hook.

He stared at me. "Why not?"

"Because!" I sounded just like Valerie.

"Mindy." He started down from the rock. It suddenly dawned on me how much bigger he was, stronger, and there was no one to hear me scream. So I started running.

"Mindy!" He yelled, but I didn't hear any footsteps coming after me. I wasn't taking any chances, though. I tore up the steps and ran blindly down a road. I wasn't even sure where I was until I recognized Aunt Margie's cottage.

Out of breath, my whole body shaking, I banged on the front door. A moment later, Joannie stepped onto the porch. "What's the matter with you?"

My insides were like a soda bottle that had been shaken. If I opened my mouth, would everything come spraying out? "That boy I was with . . . he tried to . . . you know . . ." I couldn't even say it.

But Joannie wasn't stupid. She figured out what I was trying to explain. "What exactly did he do?"

I took a deep breath. Then I gave her the details. Joannie rolled her eyes.

"Oh, for crying out loud. You're acting like he tried to rape you or something."

Okay, I didn't expect comfort and warmth from her. But I wasn't prepared for the look of amusement on her face.

I felt like a little kid who had been called off the playground for not playing nice. "It's your own fault," Joannie said. "What were you doing with a guy that old anyway? I'll bet you told him you were older, right?"

Head down, I nodded.

"I saw the way you were acting with him. You can't blame him for coming on to you. And if that's going to freak you out, you better go back to making sand castles."

Then David came out of the house with Larry and another girl. "What's going on?" David asked.

"Mindy's hysterical 'cause some boy kissed her," Joannie said.

"It was more than that!" I retorted.

"That guy you were with at the dance?" David asked.

I looked up and nodded. What a variety of expressions I saw. Joannie was clearly bored. The other girl looked like she was going to start laughing. Larry's face was sympathetic. David appeared concerned. And suddenly I felt like I was eight years old and had just fallen off a bicycle.

David grimaced. "That's disgusting. This guy must be a real sicko. You're just a kid." He turned to Larry. "Let's go back to the dance and see if we can find this guy." As the boys stepped off the porch, Joannie and her friend gazed after them in dismay.

"Damn," Joannie muttered. Then she glanced at me. "You want us to walk you home?" she asked without any enthusiasm.

"No thanks," I replied. "Believe it or not, I'm allowed to cross streets by myself now." And with as

much dignity as I could muster under the circumstan-
ces, I walked away.

I was sitting on the beach the next day in my
usual spot when I saw Patrick. He was wearing sunglasses, so I couldn't tell if he saw me.

But he turned my way, and I stiffened. Then he
took off his sunglasses. I'd never seen a real black eye
before.

"Your cousin looks out for you," he said.

I was too shocked to respond.

"Look," he said, "if I'd known you were only
thirteen, I wouldn't have tried anything. You
shouldn't have led me on like that." Then he moved
on.

I just sat there and stared out at the water. A
moment later, Jeff appeared. "Hey, I just found out
they got a pottery wheel over at the community center.
You want to go make a bowl or something?"

I shaded my eyes and looked up at him. "Jeff,
what's the name of the middle 'Brady Bunch' boy?"

"Peter."

"Oh, right." I got up. "Yeah, let's go make a
bowl." At least I'd have something to show for the
summer.

Chapter 9

*I*t was almost over. Any minute now, the rabbi would be blowing the shofar, the big curved horn that signaled the end of the Day of Atonement. And if I was hungry before, I was starving now. My food fantasies were getting bigger and more detailed. It wasn't just pizza anymore. It was pizza with pepperoni and mushrooms and peppers, maybe even the Supreme Deluxe with seven toppings.

I thought I'd feel better by now. I'd confessed, over and over and over. I'd thought about my sins, and how sorry I was that I'd committed them. I'd repented and atoned. And I'd assumed that by the end of the service, I'd feel cleansed, purified, free of guilt.

But I was still feeling crummy. And I knew why.

It wasn't because my stomach was growling.

It was something else. Something I didn't know before I came today. Even though I'd been to these services before, I'd never really listened. I came here thinking all I had to do was fast and pray, and that would take care of everything. But there was more to it. The rabbi told us several times.

I could still hear his words. "Yom Kippur does not atone for transgressions between one person and other persons. There will be atonement only when amends are made and forgiveness is obtained from the wronged party."

It figured. I should have guessed I wasn't going to get off this easy.

The blast of the shofar filled the room. The service was finished. The Day of Atonement was over. But not for me.

I eased my way through the crowds in the aisle, trying not to push or shove. Finally, I emerged outside. Since it would be dark after services, my mother had insisted on picking me up. I scanned the cars in front of the synagogue. She wasn't there yet. So I leaned against the railing at the bottom of the steps and watched the stream of unfamiliar faces go by.

And then I saw a familiar one. Marsha Greene. She was standing at the top of the steps, looking hungry and impatient and tapping her foot.

She was the first Club girl I'd seen since June, when school got out. I'd been dreading running into them when high school began for real on Monday. We'd been in orientation for the last week and none of them were in my group. And I knew it was going to be awkward when I saw any of them in classes or in the hallways.

I figured I might as well get one encounter over with now. So I kept looking at her until she turned my way and our eyes met.

To my surprise, she didn't look embarrassed at all. She waved and came down the stairs. "Hi," she said. "How was your summer?"

"Not bad. How was yours?"

"Great. I went to dance camp."

"I didn't know you dance."

"Yeah, I've been taking ballet three times a week ever since I was seven."

Funny how little I knew about one of the people I'd tried so hard to impress all year. I didn't even know she was Jewish.

"That's why I was never at the mall on Saturdays," she explained. "Ballet classes."

The mall made me think of The Club. I changed the subject. "Did you get that information pamphlet from the high school?"

She nodded. "Wasn't it neat? I can't wait. Did you see all the activities they have? There's a club that puts on musicals."

I'd noticed that, too. "I want to try out for that. I can't dance, but I like to sing."

"It's the opposite for me," Marsha said. "I'd like to get into it, too, but I'll bet it takes up a lot of time, with rehearsals and all."

That wasn't a concern for me. I figured I'd have plenty of free time. It wasn't like I had any friends.

But for Marsha . . . "Yeah, I guess it would be hard if you have ballet three times a week. And," I forced it out. "The Club."

"Mmm. I don't think The Club's going to take much time. We probably won't even be getting together that much. There's so much else to do in high school. And clubs like that, they're kind of a kid thing, y'know?"

Was she saying The Club would be breaking up? I wouldn't mind seeing that happen. But now that the subject was out in the open, I had to ask.

"Marsha . . . how come I didn't get in?"

Marsha's forehead wrinkled. "I don't remember. Oh, here come my parents. You need a ride?"

"No thanks. There's my mother now. I'll see you at school."

"How was the service?" my mother asked as I got into the car.

I fastened my seat belt. "Okay."

"Hungry?"

"Yeah."

"Why don't we stop and pick up a pizza?"

"Great."

We rode in silence. I always said my mother had eyes in the back of her head. Now I decided she had another set, just above her right ear, looking directly at me.

Well, I was going to have to start somewhere. But there was something I had to know first. "Is there a statute of limitations on getting into trouble?"

"*What?*"

"You know. Like with criminals. If you steal something, they can't prosecute you if they don't catch you within a certain length of time."

She stopped at a red light. However many sets of eyes she had, they were all on me. "Mindy! You didn't—"

"No, I didn't steal anything. I was just using that as an example. What I want to know is, what's going to happen to me if I tell you about something I did a long time ago that I wasn't supposed to do?"

I could have sworn she actually looked frightened. "What did you do?"

"Light's green," I pointed out.

It was easier to talk when the real eyes weren't searching my face. "Remember last January, when you and Dad went to that wedding in New Jersey and stayed the night?"

She nodded.

"And when you came back, the lamp in the den was gone. And I said I'd tripped against it and broke it."

There was another nod.

"That wasn't true." And I told her about the party.

When I finished, I waited for an explosion. Or a

lecture. Or both. Instead, I got silence for a few minutes as she absorbed the enormity of my act.

I couldn't blame her for being stunned. It was, after all, a multilayered sin. Having friends over without permission. Letting strangers into the house. Beer and pot. Bribing Valerie not to tell.

"Drugs," she murmured.

"Just pot. But I know that's wrong," I added quickly. "That's why I made them leave."

Her mouth was set in a tight line. What else could I tell her? "I'm sorry. And I won't ever do it again."

There was more silence. What was she thinking? Was her brain hard at work, devising some cruel and unusual punishment?

"Why are you suddenly telling me this now?" she asked.

"It was one of the sins I had to atone for today."

"*One* of the sins?"

How much more trouble could I get into? "Well, there was the time in October when you let me buy some clothes, but only if you could return them. And I bought clothes on sale, so you couldn't, even if you didn't like them. I did it on purpose. I'm sorry for that, too."

She didn't say anything, and I started feeling annoyed. What did she want me to do, beg for forgiveness? "I *said* I'm sorry."

"I heard you."

"So do you forgive me?"

"I don't know what to say. You know what you did was wrong. Especially the party."

"Of course I know. That's why I'm telling you." I still had to make amends, but I wasn't sure how. "Do you want me to save my allowance and pay for the lamp?"

"I'm not thinking about the lamp."

"Will you tell Dad? I mean, having the party was a sin against both of you."

She paused at a stop sign and turned to me. "I guess it's enough that you told me. I think I can speak for both of us." She gazed at me thoughtfully. "You haven't confided in me in a long time."

"You can go, Mom. There's nobody coming."

She didn't move. And to my amazement, she actually smiled at me. She was still looking a little bewildered and confused, but she was definitely smiling. I smiled back. Behind us, a car pulled up and honked.

We rode along in comfortable silence, and I leaned back in my seat. She didn't say anything more about my confession. And I didn't think it was because she was overwhelmed by how terrible it was. She was probably just in a state of shock because I had actually told her about it.

There were no spaces in front of the pizza take-out place so she had to double-park. "I'll have to stay in the car." She reached into her purse and handed me a bill. I hopped out of the car and went inside.

It wasn't a restaurant, just take-out, but there

were a lot of people hanging around waiting for their pizzas. I went up to the counter, placed my order, and received a number.

Then I saw her. With her frizzy red hair, she stood out in the crowd. She was leaning against the wall with a girl I'd never seen before. Having just gone through one atonement, I wasn't sure if I was up for another right away.

I took a deep breath, squared my shoulders, and went across the room. "Hi, Flip."

I half expected her to turn away and pretend I wasn't there. She certainly didn't seem overjoyed to see me. But she did say, "Hi, Mindy." And after a moment, she added, "This is Lee Hudson. Lee, this is Mindy Wise."

Lee was barely taller than me, skinny, with big wire-rimmed glasses. She didn't look like The Club type. "Hi, Mindy," she said.

"Hi. Uh, are you new in town?"

"No, I went to Lakewood." That was one of the two other middle schools in Fox Haven.

Flip spoke. "We met in summer school."

"What were you doing in summer school?"

I caught a glimpse of the old Flip. "I flunked algebra, so I had to make it up. I probably would have been taking science, too, if you hadn't gotten me through that exam."

A voice from the counter called, "Thirty-two."

"That's us," Lee said. "I'll get it."

"How was your summer?" I asked Flip.

She shrugged. "Lousy. Summer school stinks." Then she lowered her voice. "But I got my period."

I could feel the blush creeping up my neck. Here was my chance. "Flip, I'm sorry I told the others about that. I shouldn't have done it. It just sort of slipped out."

She shrugged again. I wasn't sure what that meant.

Lee returned with a big flat box. "I checked to make sure they only put anchovies on half. It was nice meeting you, Mindy."

"Same here," I replied.

The voice at the counter yelled, "Thirty-four." I checked my ticket. "That's mine. See ya."

Flip turned toward the door, but then she looked over her shoulder back at me. "Lee and I are going to the mall tomorrow. Want to come?"

She spoke in an offhand sort of way, but no invitation had ever sounded so sweet. "Yeah. I'd like to. Should I meet you around one?"

Flip nodded. "In front of the record store."

I picked up my pizza, brought it out to the car, and we drove home. As soon as we walked in the house, Valerie snatched the box from my hands. "It's about time. I'm starving."

"You're starving?" I followed her into the kitchen, where my father was setting the little table. "I've been fasting all day."

"That's dumb," Valerie said.

"No, it's not," my father said. "You fast on Yom Kippur to afflict your soul. That way you can concentrate on your transgressions."

Those were almost the exact words the rabbi had used. I looked at my father in surprise. "How'd you know that?" I asked him.

"I used to go every year," he said.

"Why don't you go anymore?" I asked.

"Because he hasn't committed any sins," Valerie answered for him. "Not like *you*."

My parents looked at each other. "That's not true, Val," he said. "We all do things we're sorry for, that we shouldn't have done. It's part of being human."

"Nobody's perfect," I added.

My father nodded. "If we were all perfect, we wouldn't need a day like Yom Kippur."

"And Catholics wouldn't need to go to confession," my mother said.

"We wouldn't even have expressions like, 'I'm sorry,' or 'forgive me,' " my father added.

My sister was looking at us as if we'd all lost our minds at the same time.

"For your information, dork, Yom Kippur is the most important day in the year for Jews," I informed her. "And I had a very meaningful religious experience."

I caught my parents giving each other a look. But

164

it wasn't The Look. There was no eye-rolling, no head-shaking. I could have sworn they actually respected what I was saying. Incredible, but true.

The pizza smelled wonderful. I was dying to tear into it. But there was something I had to do first before I could really enjoy it.

I went to the phone and dialed. "Hi, Peggy, it's Mindy."

"Hi."

"How was gymnastics camp?"

"Fine. How was your summer?"

"Fine."

"Mindy, the pizza's going to get cold," my mother said.

I spoke rapidly into the receiver. "Listen, I can't talk because we're getting ready to eat, but I just wanted to know if you could go to the mall tomorrow with me and Flip and a friend of hers."

There was silence on the other end. "Peggy? Are you there?"

"You want me to go to the mall with you?"

"Yeah. Please?"

She spoke slowly. "Okay. I need some clothes for school anyway."

"Great. I'll call you in the morning." I hung up. I hadn't said I was sorry yet. That would have to wait for the right moment, when we could be alone. But I'd started to make amends. That was something.

I've eaten a zillion pizzas in my life. But I've never had one that tasted so good.

I should be asleep. It's been a long day. But I'm lying here in bed, looking up at the ceiling, and not feeling sleepy at all.

Have I dealt with all my sins? My mother, Peggy, Flip. There was the time I allowed Dani to cheat off my social studies quiz. But that sin only hurt me. I think I covered those sins in the synagogue.

And there was Patrick, at the beach. Maybe he shouldn't have tried what he did, but in all honesty, it was my fault for leading him on and using him to act older. I couldn't do anything about that now, though. Just chalk it up to experience.

All in all, I've got a clean slate. And that's nice, because I'm on the verge of a new beginning. Next week, classes will be starting. A new school, new friends, new experiences. New chances, possibilities, opportunities.

New sins to commit. Not that I'm *planning* to do anything I'll be sorry for. But you never know. Like I said at dinner, nobody's perfect.

And as waves of drowsiness begin to envelop me, I can't help but wonder what I'll be atoning for this time next year.